Stone Wings

The Gargoyles of Arrington, Book 1

Jenn Burke

For Annabeth

Chapter 1

Josh

I eyed a flyer bunched in with the rest of the mail. It was a thin piece of poster board—or a thick piece of paper—and it looked as though someone had painstakingly written out their message, in uniform, clear inked lettering. It was a generic message that *We buy homes! For top dollar! In your area!* Okay, number one, using that many exclamation points convinced me it was one step shy of a scam. And number two—

"Do you think they actually wrote each of these flyers? Manually?" I handed the piece of paper over to Teague, who was sitting on the wood and steel barstool on the other side of the kitchen island.

He gave it a cursory glance, his spade-tipped tail swaying casually behind him, and his stone teeth grinding the hell out of his Mini Wheats. One wouldn't think a gargoyle needed a high-fiber breakfast, but that would just show how little people knew about gargoyles. Fiber was important for *everyone*. He licked a stray droplet of milk off one of his protruding lower tusks and shook his head. "No. It's too consistent."

1

I figured he'd know, as a cop. Since we weren't planning on selling the sprawling, custom-built mansion anytime soon, no matter what ridiculous price we could get, I tossed the flyer into the recycling bin. "Second shift tonight?"

Teague grunted an affirmative.

"I'll bring your lunch to the station at the regular time."

His luminous purple eyes narrowed. "You know you don't need to do that."

I waved off his protest. It was something I'd started a couple of years after becoming the gargoyles' caretaker and personal assistant, a role my dad had filled before me. It was what my family had done for centuries. Ever since these men saved my great-great-great-ad-infinitum grandparents from drowning when their ship sank as it was crossing the Atlantic from Europe. You'd think creatures made of stone would not be good life preservers, but you'd be wrong. They were probably in their mostly human form at the time, so...

At any rate, when I found out Teague was surviving primarily on coffee and donuts—way to hold up the stereotype, man—I'd started bringing him a hot, homecooked meal every shift. It wasn't like it was a hardship. It was a ten-minute drive to the station, and although everyone he worked with thought it was weird at first, I'd noticed that more and more of his colleagues started bringing their own containers of homemade goodness for their lunch breaks. See, I was a trendsetter.

I tossed an envelope with a bill on the "to be paid" pile, and couldn't hold in a groan at the next bit of mail in my hands.

"What?" Before I registered that Drew, one of Teague's younger brothers, had joined us, he'd plucked the postcard out of my hand between the claws of his forefinger and thumb. He scanned it, then grinned, showing every one of his pointed teeth. Unlike Teague, Drew didn't have tusks, but a row of shark-like daggers filling his mouth. His features were more feline, and he also had wings, which, as far as I knew, couldn't support him in the air—they were for show only. I'd always wondered if he was disappointed in that.

"Your high school reunion is coming up?" he asked incredulously.

I couldn't look at him, but instead tidied the piles of mail that didn't need any tidying. "I'm not going."

"Why not?" Teague asked around a mouthful of fiber.

Ugh. How could I explain? The brothers had never attended high school—they had zero concept of modern day education except for what they'd watched on TV. Which, to be fair, was both horrible and not horrible enough. Sometimes when someone got bullied, there was no magical glow-up that showed everyone they were wrong, that the person was smart and handsome and worth their attention. And it wasn't even that I was really bullied. I mean, I'd dated one of the most popular guys in school, and I hadn't been ugly by any stretch of the imagination. But I just hadn't *fit*, probably because I had this huge secret I could never share with anyone. I'd always known there was more to the world than the rest of my classmates even suspected, and that had made me a little weird. My uber-popular high-school boyfriend Brandon made sure I realized, over and over again, that he was doing me a favor by being with me.

"There's a reason I don't have any friends from high school."

Teague grunted.

Drew rolled his eyes at his brother. "They were assholes, huh?"

It never failed to impress me that the gargoyles had so

3

quickly adapted to modern language. For only having been awake for twenty-three years—this time—they'd managed to pick up the lingo pretty well. But I guess they had to be incredibly good at adapting to their circumstances to survive the curse without going mad.

One hundred years asleep, twenty five awake, until they broke the curse. It was some true love nonsense that would do it. Or, well, maybe not nonsense because one of the brothers had managed to break the curse the last time they were awake. According to their youngest surviving brother, Rian—who was probably off researching somewhere this morning—it had been love at first sight for Finnian, when he'd seen Elizabeth walking down the main street of Arrington, British Columbia, when the town was made up of barely more than a tavern, a general store and a warehouse. Despite the era demanding women dress a certain way, Elizabeth had been scandalous in a man's shirt and trousers, her hair braided down her back, smile wide and eyes sparkling as her father made her laugh. Finnian had fallen head over heels at that moment, and though it had been a rough ride to their happily-ever-after, they'd achieved it and —boom—curse broken.

I knew the brothers were happy he escaped their torment, but their eyes were always a little sad when they spoke of him.

With a sigh, I shrugged. "High school sucked."

Teague frowned, his pronounced brow wrinkling. "Didn't you have a boyfriend in high school?"

Of course he'd remember that. I evened out the edges of the stack of mail in front of me. "I did."

"And he broke up with you."

I looked up with an exasperated sigh. "Thanks, Teague.

Glad you could help me revisit one of the most embarrassing moments of my life."

Whose boyfriend breaks up with them on prom night? Mine, apparently. Like, *at* prom. In the middle of the slow dance right after Brandon had been crowned Prom King.

Ugh.

"So that's why you don't want to go." Teague, as always, was way too perceptive.

"Can you blame me?"

Drew tapped the postcard. "It says you can bring a plus-one."

"You might have noticed that I have a distinct lack of plus-one candidates at the moment."

One of his wings lifted and flexed, his version of a shrug. "I'll go."

I rolled my eyes. "Great. The only thing more embarrassing than going by myself would be to go with one of my bosses." Gathering up the mail I needed to open and deal with, I waved a hand. "It's no biggie. I don't have to go." Even if, by not going, I felt I was letting all the assholes in my past win.

I wanted nothing more than to show them all I'd succeeded. I mean, not in a *Carrie* kind of way. More in a *you knocked me down, but I got up again* sort of way. Maybe I'd even sing Chumbawamba while I was at it. That would definitely secure my reputation.

"What if I pretended to be your boyfriend?"

Drew's suggestion stopped me in my tracks at the kitchen's threshold. "If you what?"

He lifted one massive stone hand. "Hear me out."

I was so stunned by the words coming out of his mouth that I had little choice.

"You do so much for us. You manage the household

5

stuff. You look after the finances, including those of my and Rian's shops. You keep us on track with our schedules and nudge us when we're getting too old fashioned. Josh, I'm not kidding when I say we'd be lost without you."

"It's my job. Dad did the same thing."

"Yeah, he did, and I know he cared about us—still does," he amended quickly. "But it was never in his personality to be a caretaker like you are. You're driven."

I swallowed and looked away. I don't know why Drew's simple words affected me so hard. Maybe because so few people got that about me? Brandon certainly never had. He'd thought my desire to look after people had been a sign of a lack of ambition—which was why he'd broken up with me. He couldn't hitch himself to someone who wasn't permanently striving for the biggest salary. Something he'd apparently realized only after we were at prom.

"So let us do this for you," Drew continued. "It's one night, and I'll bet most of your classmates don't even live in town anymore, right?"

Yeah, they'd all abandoned Arrington for the glamour of the big city, either Vancouver or Toronto. Some had settled for Calgary. At least, that's what I knew from Facebook. Not that I stalked their profiles or anything.

Okay, maybe after I'd had too much wine. But that wasn't often.

He saw me wavering, and continued, his grin widening. "It's not like we'll have to reveal that we're pretending. C'mon. It'll be fun."

I couldn't help picturing Drew, dressed up and standing beside me in his human form. Could I get him into a suit? Probably not—the man had discovered jeans and lived in them when he was in his mostly human skin. But maybe a sports coat? A button-down that was open at the neck? His blond hair slightly mussed as it always was, and his piercing light-blue eyes under his thick, dark brows seemingly looking into people's souls as they approached. I could picture it too easily, not that I'd ever admit it. I *might* have spent a little time thinking about Drew as I was growing up. Um, and after I took over from Dad. But I'd quickly shoved all those thoughts aside so I could be what the brothers needed me to be. A professional. The buffer between them and the outside world.

And now he was offering to be the same for me. How could I say no?

I smiled. "Okay, sure. It's a date."

He raised a brow, and for a second, I wanted to die. Why had I said that? A date? But his grin only widened. "Bring it on."

Chapter 2

Drew

"Ow, shit. That hurt." I glared at my little brother, Rian, and he shot a smirk back at me as the tattoo gun started buzzing again.

"You big baby." He shook his head. "You'd think with the amount of ink I've done on you over the years, you'd be used to it."

He wasn't wrong. My chest and stomach bore so many tattoos—mostly black, but with some color here and there. Designs I'd chosen, and some Rian had, like the one he was currently etching into my skin—some sort of rune. At first, I'd wondered if the ink would appear in my stone form as well. The fun designs didn't, but Rian's runes did, as though they'd been carved by a stone mason. That was his talent.

When we'd first awoken after being cursed and discovered we were no longer human, we also found that we each had a talent. I could manipulate metal and reshape it into anything I wished, simply with the power of thought. Teague could sense someone's emotional state, which made him an excellent lie detector, a definite plus in his chosen line of work. And Rian was able to imbue runes with magic

8

and intent, turning the symbols into powerful triggers that could do anything from protect someone or something, to other, more drastic actions, such as hurting someone. I bore a few of his runes, none of which had worked as he hoped to end the curse. He had even more decorating his arms, shoulders and chest, plus his back had a full, amazing piece depicting a sunrise with five silhouettes—Rian, Teague and myself, plus our two other brothers, Finnian and Odhrán. It might not be as magical as his runes, but it was magical in its own way. It represented hope that we'd see our lost brothers again.

I pushed away the past and refocused on the present. Dwelling never solved anything. "So what's this one supposed to do?"

Rian paused and wiped away excess ink and blood with a paper towel. He'd stenciled the rune in a relatively blank spot on my ribs, a spot that was more than a little painful. His vibrantly red hair peeked out from the backwards-facing brim of the hooligan hat that he wore to cover the remnants of the horns he sawed away whenever he switched from his living stone skin to his human skin. It was a pain in the ass, but at least he could do something about them. Me, I was stuck with folding my wings as tightly as I could against my back, wearing baggy or boxy clothing, and hoping people didn't notice.

That was the thing about our curse. On top of our magical talents, even when we were in our human form, we were always reminded that we weren't fully human, not anymore. I had my wings, Rian had his horns, and Teague had his tail. I'd take it, though; it was better than when we'd awoken for the first time after being cursed and couldn't find our human forms at all. Those had been frightening years.

"It should fortify your will." Before I could ask exactly what that meant, he continued, "Make it easier for you to stay in your human skin for longer periods. If it works, then I can build on it." He bent back to his art, and the gun started buzzing again. "I think the reason the other ones didn't work is that I was expecting them to do too much. We need to take smaller steps."

I thought the reason the other ones didn't work was because the runes were a fool's hope, but I didn't say that to Rian. This time around, once he'd discovered tattooing, he'd been convinced that etching magic into our skin would counteract the effects of the curse, if only he could find the right combination of symbols and runes. But here we were, with two years left before we slept for another century, and he had yet to find the key.

But dwelling on the past was fruitless, and so was dwelling on what was to come. The present was the only thing we had control over.

"I heard you're going with Josh to his...what is it? High school reunion?"

I bit back a hiss as the needle encountered a particularly sensitive spot. "Teague?"

"Of course, Teague." I could hear the smile in his voice. "He loves his gossip."

That he did. For a stoic bastard, he certainly enjoyed spreading the juiciest news. "Josh was in a bind, and he clearly wanted to go."

"But...pretending to be his boyfriend? Really?"

"It's just for one evening."

Rian paused again, going through the ritual of wiping down the area he'd been working on, and looked me in the eyes. He was quiet for a few moments as his blue eyes, a few shades darker than mine, filled with worry. If anyone looked closely, they'd see a tinge of red there, another sign of his cursed form. When he was in his stone skin, his eyes glowed a terrifying crimson.

"What?" I finally said.

He shook his head. "You're right. It's only for one evening."

Oh no, he wasn't getting off that easily. "Rian."

He pushed the brim of his cap up with his forearm. "Just...be careful, all right?"

I frowned. "Are you worried I'm going to lose my skin? It'll be after sunset, but I've got plenty of practice keeping the stone at bay." It was always harder to stay human when the sun went down, but it wasn't impossible.

"No, it's not that." He pursed his lips. "You know Josh has a crush on you, right?"

"No, he doesn't."

"Uh, yes. He does."

"You're full of shit. There's no way."

Rian rolled his eyes. "Aindréas Ó Raghallaigh, I love you, but you're an oblivious sod."

Oh, the full Irish name, was it? We'd anglicized our names when we'd emigrated to North America. I'd become Andrew O'Reilly—Drew for short—but every once in a while, my full name appeared on one of my brothers' lips, if only to make a point.

Apparently, today, the point was that I was something of a dupe.

"You don't know what you're talking about," I insisted. Because, seriously, Josh having a crush on me was ludicrous. I'd watched him grow up. I was a few *hundred* years his senior. Oh, and let's not forget that in two years, I would turn into a statue and sleep for a century. Such a catch, I was. Totally worthy of a crush. *Not.*

Rian shook his head and got back to inking my skin. "Fine. I know nothing. Ignore me."

"I usually do."

"But I'm going to help you find the right outfit for the reunion."

I narrowed my eyes. "I can dress myself perfectly well."

He pointedly looked me up and down. "You sure about that?"

"I'm dressed for work!" There was no point in wearing good clothes when I'd likely get oil on them or rip them—I'd done both in the past. My ragged jeans and worn T-shirt worked fine, thank you very much.

"Uh-huh."

"Scut."

"Gobdaw."

"Minger."

I laughed. "I love you, brother."

He smiled at me fondly. "Same."

THERE WAS nothing quite like working on a misty day. It was cool, but warm enough that I could have the garage doors open while I banged away at my latest project, a 1970 Buick Riviera. I'd asked Alexa to play a classic rock playlist and there was no one else in the shop right now to challenge my choice, since my apprentice, Karma—yes, that was her actual name—was off today.

I was still amazed at how significantly the world had changed this go-round. Every time we'd awoken, there was some new thing to gawk at, but this time, there were so many advances it was a wonder any of us had been able to adapt. I couldn't believe how cars had changed. That people now flew across oceans with the same blasé attitude that I'd felt riding a wagon into the closest village. That astronauts had been to the *moon*, and scientists wanted to conquer Mars next. It was enough to explode one's brain, it was.

The little things thrilled me. Such as the changes in music, the technology that eased everyone's lives—perhaps complicated them as well, but we wouldn't dwell on that—and the complete access to knowledge everyone now had.

But what excited me the most? Cars.

When we'd last gone to sleep in 1899, motor vehicles were brand new. Spindly things, they could barely go faster than a horse could trot and had no personality to amuse you. I'd thought they'd be the toys of the rich and nothing more. Imagine my shock when I awoke in 1999 to find cars everywhere. All shapes, sizes, and colors. Sedans and vans for families, trucks for laborers, giant trucks for transporting goods, sporty things with no other purpose than to look good while you went fast. Faster than I could have ever imagined. When Josh's dad, Henry, had taken us on a highway for the first time in his plain family sedan, I'd shouted in joy.

And thus my love affair.

I'd always been mechanically inclined, so it was natural that my newfound love would lead me to be a mechanic for these incredible creations. In 2010, I opened Stone Wing Motors and focused on doing what I loved most—repairing and restoring powerful cars from the 1960s and 1970s, the ones that roared when you stepped on the gas and were not at all like the wimpy little things I'd known in the nineteenth century, nor the very civilized vehicles that were popular today. So few of these beauties remained, and I longed to see them in their glory, as I never had when they were new.

It would be one of the things I'd miss most when I went to sleep this time.

No, not going there. Staying in the present was the only way to stay sane.

The throaty rumble of a motorcycle distracted me from my work. Hearing them in the summer was no surprise, but at this time of year—mid-October—they were less common. Though we didn't get the snow in the British Columbia interior that the rest of Canada did, in autumn it did get down to nearly freezing at night, and the days had a bite of winter to them when you weren't in the sun.

I pushed myself out from under the heap that would eventually be a gorgeous boat of a car, stood, and automatically grabbed the rag out of my back pocket to wipe my hands. On the other side of the open garage door was an unfamiliar man on a gleaming Harley. He'd turned it off and watched me from behind a pair of mirrored aviator sunglasses. Seeing as the sun had yet to burn through the mist, I immediately classified him as a—what was the term Josh used? Oh yes. Douchebag. He wore a black leather jacket that looked decades old, worn jeans, and a pair of battered combat boots. His dirty-blond hair was longer than mine, pulled back into a tail at the nape of his neck, and he sported a beard that wasn't quite full but far more than stubble. There was no helmet in sight, which solidified my initial impression that he was indeed a douchebag.

He jerked his chin in my direction as I stepped beyond the threshold of my garage. "You O'Reilly?"

"One of them. Can I help you?"

He grinned, his teeth gleaming white. "Nah. Just checking out the competition."

Competition? I hadn't heard about another garage opening nearby. Besides, with a population of close to twenty-five thousand, Arrington had plenty of customers to go around. I didn't worry about losing business—not that it would matter in a couple of years, anyway. I tucked the rag back into my coveralls. "You're new to the area, then?"

The man flipped out his kickstand and dismounted. "Me and my pride, yeah."

Oh. *That* kind of competition.

It wasn't the first time we'd encountered folks who wanted to encroach on our territory. Not that my brothers and I truly thought of Arrington as our territory—we weren't like the other shifters we'd met, who claimed territory for their pack or pride and patrolled it to keep it under their control. Territory was everything to them, and they were more animal than human, even in their two-legged form.

Mind you, my perception might be somewhat tainted since the last time we'd trusted a pack of shifters, we'd awoken from our century-long sleep to find our youngest brother, Odhrán, as nothing more than fragments of stone and dust.

Perhaps it wasn't fair to hold that against all shifters, but it was difficult to be objective in the face of losing a loved one.

He continued grinning as he approached me, pushing his sunglasses to the top of his head. Up close, he was taller than I expected, a good two or three inches more than my five-foot-ten. Lifting his nose, he gave the air an obvious sniff, no doubt catching the scent of my annoyance. "Yeah, I heard you and your brothers don't like shifters much."

Especially not douchebag asshats. "There are plenty of better environments for yourself and your pride. Arrington is too urban for the likes of you."

"I'm not blind, dipshit. There's good work to be had,

though, and hunting grounds nearby. It's exactly what we need." His tawny eyes glittered. "You need to stay out of our way."

"Or?" I squared my shoulders.

He shifted back onto his heels. "I've heard lots about you and your brothers, O'Reilly. All the packs and prides in BC thought you guys were nothing more than legends until you showed up in 1999. Did you know a couple of packs considered you the harbingers of the apocalypse?" He chuckled and shook his head. "People thought weird shit about the turn of the millennium. But the rumors say you're awake for, what, twenty-five years? Then you go to sleep again. So you can bitch about us being here all you want, but I figure all I need to do is wait you out. It won't be too much longer, and you'll be gone. So here's my deal—you stay out of our way and when you go to sleep, we'll leave you alone."

I gritted my teeth. "You fecking gobshite."

The man tipped his head back with a bark of laughter. "Nice! I love it."

He turned his back on me—which, for a shifter, was as good as saying I wasn't worth his concern—and headed back to his bike. "Name's Becker, by the way," he said casually as he knocked the bike's kickstand back into place. "You'll be seeing more of me."

"I'd better fecking not."

He laughed again. "We're gonna be good neighbors, O'Reilly."

I glared as he fired up his Harley, flipped his sunglasses down, and roared away.

Good neighbors? Over my dead body, we would.

Chapter 3

Josh

I t was ridiculous that I was so nervous. Ugh. No matter how much I tried to tell myself that it didn't matter what everyone at this stupid reunion thought of me, I couldn't shake the anxiety in my gut. This whole thing was going to be about judgment, like I was some beauty pageant contestant stepping out on stage in front of a panel of judges who would evaluate me based on my appearance and success—or lack thereof, in their minds.

Why was I going to this thing again?

A low whistle startled me. I spun to find Rian, in his stone skin, wearing nothing but a pair of athletic joggers. In this form, he had intricate horns jutting from his head, and his arms were covered in runes that he'd tattooed onto his human skin. His facial features were narrower than his brothers', and he looked more like the classical renditions of the devil.

"Lookin' good, Josh." He gave me a thumbs-up and a smile, revealing his upper and lower fangs. "That's a good color on you."

I'd worried that the emerald-green suit would be too

much, but it *was* my color, and I refused to drab myself down for any occasion, except a funeral. But that was neither here nor there. "Thanks. Do you know if Drew's ready?"

Footsteps clomped down the stairs, Drew's voice preceding his appearance. "I'm ready."

It was a good thing he hadn't asked me a question because...I'd forgotten how to form words. He was wearing a *suit.* I didn't know which brother had gotten him to buy one, but I owed them.

If I'd thought Drew was hot in his usual oil-stained jeans and coveralls, it was nothing compared to how he looked in a suit. The suit wasn't an eye-catching hue like mine, but it didn't need to be. The way the slate fabric hugged Drew's shoulders, arms, and legs...the way his simple white shirt was open at the neck, drawing attention to his collarbone and the tiny bit of ink visible from the tattoos on both of his pecs...the way his long legs were capped in a pair of glossy leather boots...it was enough to make people drool.

Me. I was people.

Drew paused midstep as he took in my unwavering gaze. His blond hair had been tamed somewhat, but still appeared artfully messy, and his short, brown beard looked glossy and soft. "Am I overdressed? Goddammit, Rian, I told you. This is too much."

"No." The word came out choked, so I cleared my throat and tried again. "You look great. You're perfect. I mean"—shit—"the outfit is perfect."

"Yeah, Drew, see?" Rian leaned on the kitchen island, smirking. "You're perfect."

I was tempted to smack him, but seeing as he was in

stone, that would not turn out well for me. Instead, I nervously tugged at my suit jacket.

"You look great too," Drew said. "The green is great. And the cut is..."

"Great?" Rian interjected, grinning now.

"Shut up," Drew and I said in unison.

He laughed. "Okay, okay. Have fun tonight. Be good."

Drew lifted his thumb to his mouth and flicked it in Rian's direction, which only made Rian laugh louder. "Wanker," Drew muttered at Rian's retreating form, before turning back to me. "Truly, you look wonderful. I especially like the tie."

Of course, I had to look down to catch a glimpse, even though I already knew what it looked like. It was a paisley pattern on a black background, with bits of green that matched the suit, as well as blue, gold, and a splash of yellow and red. I'd paired it with a pale green shirt, and I thought I looked sharp as hell. Maybe not as good as Drew did, though.

"Thanks." I angled my head around to his back and was surprised that I couldn't tell he had wings. "I didn't realize you could fold your wings down that tightly."

He grimaced. "I've got them strapped down."

"That can't be comfortable."

"Eh, I've experienced worse."

I bounced onto my toes and back, feeling suddenly awkward. He seemed to have the same issue, since he looked everywhere but at me. How the hell were we going to pull off this fake dating thing?

Oh. We should probably talk about that. "We might need to, uh, be affectionate. To pull this off."

"Like, what? Kissing?"

I tried to ignore the note of horror in his voice. "No, not kissing. But maybe holding hands. If you're okay with that?"

"Right, sure." He shot me a fleeting grin. "No problem."

"If you don't want to go, no hard feelings. I promise."

"It's not that. It's—" He shook his head. "Little touches. I can do that."

I thought about offering him another out, but honestly, I didn't want to. I *wanted* to go. I wanted to show off this gorgeous man and pretend, for one night, that he was mine. That wouldn't hurt anyone.

Except maybe me. But I was a big boy. I could keep a handle on my emotions and not let them get carried away in the fantasy.

I pushed down my worries and smiled. "Great. We don't need to make anything up. Everyone knows my family has always worked for yours, so we can simply say the feelings developed over time."

"Easy enough. For our first date, I took you on a picnic."

That took me off guard and suggested a romantic depth to Drew that I'd never guessed at. "That sounds nice."

"Yeah? Good."

"I think it should be recent that we've started dating. That way, it won't be a shock that no one's heard about it."

"Right. And if anyone questions it later, we can say it didn't end up working out, but we're still friends."

I nodded. "It sounds like we've got a plan."

"That it does." Drew held out his elbow. "Shall we head to our doom? I mean, your reunion?"

I threaded my arm through his, grinning. At least he held no illusions that this was going to be fun. "Lead on, Mr. O'Reilly."

THE REUNION REMINDED me of every high school dance I'd ever attended. For those counting at home, that would be two: one in Grade 9 in the hopes I'd make friends and fit in —spoiler: it didn't happen—and prom, where my boyfriend of two years broke up with me after being crowned prom king. It was crowded, lit sporadically with a strobe light, and the music was far too loud. The only real difference was that we were in a hotel event room instead of the high school gym.

Most people seemed to have chosen a style between business casual and formal. I spotted two women in gowns reminiscent of prom dresses, but most wore more comfortable clothing. Some men wore suits, but plenty were in jeans and sportscoats or polos. Guess we could have dressed down a little.

I shot Drew an apologetic glance, but he wasn't looking at me. Instead, he was surveying the room as though he were some sort of king observing his people, though I was pretty sure he wasn't actually royalty. Nobility, maybe, but I'd never asked and, surprisingly, it wasn't knowledge that had been passed down through the generations of caretakers in my family. His artistically messy hair glinted every time the strobe passed over us, and in the darkness between flashes, his brown beard looked nearly black.

"See anyone you recognize?" he asked, his eyes still on the crowd.

I jerked my gaze away from him. Right. My focus wasn't supposed to be on him. "Not yet."

Maybe it was because of the dim lighting or because ten years wrought more changes than I expected, but the mob of people was just that—a mob of unfamiliar faces. For a moment, I wondered if this whole set up was for nothing.

What did it matter who I attended with if I didn't run into anyone I knew?

As if the fates heard me, a white woman with eyes only for Drew bumped into me. The wine in her glass sloshed dangerously but came a few millimeters short of splashing onto my suit.

"I am so sorry," she gushed, but stopped abruptly when she looked up. "Wait—Joshy? Josh Pallesen?"

It took me a moment, but I was successful at placing the round blue eyes, pert nose, and curly blond hair. "Amanda Kirchner?"

"You remember me! Hi! Look at you, Joshy. Guess you finally hit your growth spurt, huh?" She beamed at me, as though we'd been best friends. Another spoiler: we'd never been friends, period. But I guess ten years could erase a lot of memories.

Not mine, though.

"Hey. Yeah." I gave her a smile, but it felt awkward and strained.

She turned to the woman with her, who I now recognized as Regina Harris, Amanda's partner in crime. Literally. They'd been caught vandalizing another girl's car in Grade 11. It figured they were still friends. "Reggie, you remember Joshy, right?"

Regina didn't even glance my way. Her brown eyes were glued to the man beside me, and a slight flush stained her pale cheeks. "Sure. But I don't think I've met *you*, Mr...."

"Drew O'Reilly," he said with a slight hint of his Irish brogue. It only came out when he was drunk or pissed—and seeing as we hadn't ventured to the bar yet, I knew which was riding him now. You wouldn't know it by looking at his smile unless you noticed it didn't touch his eyes.

"Sorry, Drew. This is Amanda Kirchner and Regina Harris."

"Nice to meet you. I'm Josh's boyfriend."

The hopeful light in Regina's eyes dimmed, but Amanda let out a piercing squeal. "Yay, Joshy, that's awesome! You must be happy to have someone in your life again."

I liked how she assumed I hadn't been with anyone since my ex broke up with me in high school. What stung more was that she wasn't completely wrong. I'd had a few boyfriends, but none of them had been worthwhile. Like, at all.

"We always thought it was awful what Brandon did," Regina said.

Amanda nodded vigorously. "I mean, everyone knew it was coming, but he should've done it before prom. At least then you wouldn't have gone and seen what you'd be missing out on. Because, you know, traditionally the prom king of Arrington West High tends to go on to be *super* successful."

I gritted my teeth. Everyone had known he was going to break up with me, had they? Had he told them, or had they all assumed I was a temporary thing? Though two years wasn't exactly temporary. It had been long enough for me to start dreaming about my future with him. After he'd dumped me, it had taken a lot of contemplating the past for me to realize I'd been nothing more than a project to him.

"Ladies, it was lovely to meet you, but Josh and I have a couple of beers with our names on them. Cheers." He hooked a hand around my elbow and tugged me away from the two women, who promptly tucked their heads together to whisper something. Probably something about me.

I told myself I didn't care. Maybe if I did that often enough, I'd start to believe it.

Drew paused about halfway to the bar and bent close to my ear. "You okay?"

"Yeah." My voice wasn't the strongest, so I firmed it before continuing. "That's probably not the only encounter we'll have like that tonight."

He let out something that sounded suspiciously like a growl. "Why did you want to come again?"

"To show them high school didn't break me."

He looked at me for a few seconds, his face unreadable. I thought maybe after meeting Amanda and Regina, he understood a little better the demons I was facing. "Beer, then. I need something to distract myself with if anyone talks shite so I don't start busting heads."

I chuckled, because I didn't think Drew would actually bust anyone's head. After a lifetime of knowing him, and five years of being around him twenty-four-seven, I *knew* him. He was a lot of bluff and bluster. Not that he wouldn't defend me if I were truly threatened, but he wouldn't meet words with fists.

It wasn't him.

AN HOUR OR SO LATER, I was forced to reevaluate what Drew might or might not do. He was absolutely seething beside me. As I'd warned him, we'd had more chats with former classmates of mine, none of which had been particularly pleasant. At least, not on our side. I doubted the people I spoke to realized how demeaning they were being.

Calling me Joshy, for example. I'd never liked that nickname because it wasn't used in affection but in an attempt to diminish me. By using that name, they were making sure I knew I was lesser, smaller.

Then there were those who asked what I was doing now. When I said I was a personal assistant, the response was some variation of: *but what are your long-term plans?* As though my job were a stepping stone, unworthy of any real devotion.

Oh, and then some used talking to me as a ruse to get close to Drew.

I could almost hear Drew grinding his teeth. But, to his credit, he didn't jump in to defend me—nothing he said would make a difference in these people's minds, and he was smart enough to know that. What he did do was even better. He snaked an arm around my waist and tugged me tight to his side. Like a real boyfriend would.

It would be easy to get used to being held by this man. Protected by him. The crush I'd mostly suppressed flared, reminding me how much I *liked* him.

It's only for one night, I reminded myself. But dammit, I was going to enjoy this one night.

At some point, they put out hors d'oeuvres, and Drew and I positioned ourselves at the edge of the crowd with our plates, people watching while we snacked. As I lifted my last canapé to my lips, the crowd parted, and I saw him.

Brandon Beattie. My ex. The one and only guy who'd broken my heart.

He was standing with a group of people, the center of attention, as always. He wore a suit too, but I couldn't tell the color—dark, maybe navy. I flashed back to prom, to the moment he looked me in the eyes, so serious, and I'd thought he was going to propose. I had never told anyone that, and looking back, I was glad I hadn't, since he'd broken up with me instead. He'd been in a dark suit then too, wearing the silly prom king crown, as he flipped my world upside down. Everything I'd dreamed about while we were dating had gone *poof* with a few heartbreaking words.

You're not who I need.

Before I could nudge Drew to another location in the large room, Brandon spotted me. His smile widened and he made a beeline toward us, a shorter, younger man trailing behind him. Their hands were clasped, and the other man smiled up at Brandon like he hung the moon.

I'd looked at him like that once. Before he'd broken my heart.

"Incoming ex," I murmured to Drew and braced myself.

Chapter 4

Drew

Josh's ex-classmates were assholes, the lot of them. Nothing they said even came close to changing the initial impression set by Amanda and Regina; in fact, every subsequent encounter solidified it. They all demeaned Josh in subtle and not-so-subtle ways. I hated how his shoulders seemed to curl in on themselves, as though each word made him smaller.

Ass. Holes.

And the biggest one of all was coming our way.

"Oh my god, Josh! You look so good!" Without even a by-your-leave, Brandon Beattie swept into Josh's personal space and wrapped him up in a hug. "How have you been?"

Josh wasn't one to shy away from affectionate displays. He didn't mind it when my brothers or I ruffled his hair, for example, or squeezed his shoulder. But I'd never seen him look so uncomfortable as he did right now, enveloped in his ex's broad arms.

Brandon was good-looking, I had to admit. He had straight medium-brown shortish hair, skin that was a shade or two lighter than tan, and he seemed fit. His teeth were white and straight, and there was only a hint of lines at the corner of his brown eyes, enough to suggest he laughed a lot. He wore dark-wash jeans paired with a maroon-and-white checkered button-down and brown suit jacket. If I saw him in the street, I'd probably spend a moment admiring the view because nothing in his appearance gave away his true nature.

"Hey." Josh cleared his throat and stumbled back a step as Brandon put him down. Side by side, Brandon dwarfed Josh in height as well as width. "Good to see you too, Brandon." He smiled, but I'm sure I was the only one who saw that it didn't reach his eyes. "This is Drew O'Reilly, my boyfriend. Drew, Brandon Beattie."

"O'Reilly?" Brandon's eyes grew distant for a moment. "Isn't that the name of the family your dad was a butler to?"

Butler. Psh. As though that title covered exactly the role members of Josh's family had held for centuries. Guardians, caretakers, protectors—those titles fit better. But modern society didn't understand that.

"Exactly," I said, holding out a hand, a fake smile plastered on my lips. Brandon didn't hesitate to shake, proving to me he had no survival instinct. "Josh's family and mine are great friends. Partners, almost. It's only natural that Josh and I connected, as it were."

Brandon's hand tightened on mine. "You're quite a bit older than he is."

My smile widened into something more genuine. *Oh, if only you knew, lad.* "A bit. But when you meet the one, you know it, don't you?"

"You do." It was the shorter man with Brandon who spoke. He had a peaches-and-cream complexion and light-blond hair tipped with blue that matched his liner-high-lighted eyes. "Hi! I'm Arie Holst, Brandon's husband."

Josh and I shook his hand, then I wrapped my arm across the small of Josh's back. It was protective of me, maybe a tad possessive, but I wanted him to know I was there for him. I wasn't sure if he had any feelings left for Brandon, but it couldn't be easy to hear Brandon had moved on so thoroughly.

"Congratulations," Josh said to Brandon. "I hadn't heard you'd gotten married."

"Well, no, you wouldn't have if you're still a homebody like you used to be." Brandon laughed. He pulled Arie close and pressed a kiss to his temple. "We've been married for two years."

"*Almost* two years," Arie corrected him. "Our anniversary is in two months."

"Close enough to say two years, love."

Something about the slight exaggeration didn't sit well with me, but maybe I was simply eager to find fault with him. "That's great," I said, my fake smile still in place.

"And how long have you two been seeing each other?" Arie prompted.

"Oh, it's fairly...fairly new," Josh said, stumbling a little over the lie.

"Sometimes love sneaks up on you," I added. "Then suddenly, one day, a switch is flipped, and you realize what you've been looking for all along is right there beside you."

Josh looked up at me, surprise written across his features. Before I knew it, I'd bent to brush a kiss across his lips.

I didn't expect the jolt I experienced as soon as our skin touched. I hadn't felt anything like it before, not even when we held hands. His lips were instantly warm and supple, as though my kiss hadn't been as much of a shock to him as it was to me. But a breath later, I forgot all about the surprising nature of my actions. Josh's lips moved, about to invite me in. Kissing Josh was...it was...

He pulled back with a subtle gasp and looked at Brandon and Arie. Our onlookers were watching us with soft eyes, as if our simple, not-long-enough kiss had melted their hearts.

Wait...I gave myself an internal shake. I had no right to be thinking *not long enough* when it came to that kiss. Or any kiss with Josh. I shouldn't be thinking about kissing Josh at all. Except...I could still feel his mouth against mine, how we'd almost kissed deeper than a peck in a public place should go. For the first time in...God, who knew how long, I felt a fire in my belly and desire in my veins.

Which was ridiculous. This was *Josh*. I could still remember the first time I'd met him, shortly after awakening this time around. He'd been all of five years old, with gaps in his teeth, unruly hair, and a penchant for digging in the yard after Rian joked about being a pirate and burying treasure somewhere on our property.

And yet...

"You're so sweet together." Arie gripped Brandon's arm. "Aren't they?"

"Yeah." Brandon grinned. "I guess I did you a favor, huh?"

The spots of color dotting Josh's cheeks grew more pronounced, but I was pretty sure the pink flush that started with our kiss was burning from anger now. I was thankful my skin didn't show my emotions like Josh's, or my cheeks would be fiery with rage too.

"So, where are you living these days?" Josh asked, completely ignoring Brandon's comment.

I thought I saw a flash of annoyance in Brandon's expression that Josh hadn't risen to his bait, but it was quickly gone. "Vancouver, right downtown. Our condo has a great view of the ocean."

"It's small," Arie added. "But we don't need that much space. It's just the two of us. I've got my studio, Brandon's got his office, and we can have dinner parties. What more do you need?"

Small, my arse. That sounded like a three-bedroom condo in the heart of Vancouver. I might be a mechanic from the Ass-End of Nowhere, BC, but I was a businessman too, and I read enough articles about real estate in the provincial news media to know *any* property in Vancouver was a stupidly expensive purchase.

Josh knew it too, but he didn't appear impressed. Point for him. "That sounds pretty sweet. I guess you're doing well for yourself."

Brandon shrugged. "Investment banker. I do okay."

Oh, the faux humility made me want to growl. I must have tensed my arm around Josh's waist because he leaned into me harder for a second. The contact immediately relaxed me—or, at least, reduced my tension.

"He does better than okay," Arie jumped in, grinning up at Brandon. "Because of him, I can focus on my designs."

"Arie's a fashion designer," Brandon explained. "He was featured in Vancouver's fashion week show last year, and this spring, he'll be debuting in New York."

"Wow." Josh's smile looked forced. "That's great."

"I'm going to take the world by storm, and it's all because I have this man standing with me." Arie leaned up and pressed a kiss to Brandon's cheek.

"How about you?" Brandon asked. "Did you ever make it out of Arrington?"

Josh's shoulders rose subtly. "No. Never felt the need to."

Jenn Burke

Brandon rolled his eyes. If he thought his smile softened the motion, he would be wrong. "Same old Josh. Never looking for more. I guess it worked out, though." He flicked his gaze in my direction.

I understood everything Brandon wasn't saying. Perhaps I was reading into his words, but I didn't think so. He felt Josh's supposed lack of ambition was related to me—an older man with enough money to have a *butler*, and here I was with Josh on my arm.

"I'm not a candy daddy," I said firmly.

"Sugar daddy," Josh whispered.

"Sugar daddy," I corrected without missing a beat. "Josh is an incredibly competent personal assistant for my brothers and me. He manages our schedules, our finances, our web presence for our businesses, and any events we hold. He's an amazing asset, and we're so lucky to have him."

"What sorts of businesses?" Arie asked, without even acknowledging what I'd said about Josh. As though the businesses we ran were more important than the man who helped us every day.

My skin flickered, a gentle reminder that my emotions had a tendency to affect my ability to stay human. I surreptitiously touched the new rune Rian had inked on my ribs, the one that was supposed to fortify my will. I wasn't sure if the touch through clothing would work, but damn, I needed some patience right now. The magic keeping me human settled after a second, but whether it was because of the rune or my own control, I didn't know.

"Drew owns Stone Wing Motors," Josh said, a definite note of pride in his voice. "He does restorations on classic cars. His brother, Rian, is a tattoo artist with his own studio, called Rune Ink. Their oldest brother, Teague, is a police officer."

They might not be the sort of white-collar career Brandon had, but our occupations suited us perfectly. Did they bring in enough money for us to live in downtown Vancouver? No, but I wouldn't want that anyway. Besides, Finnian had made sure to build on the investments we'd made each time we'd awoken. Technically, none of us had to work to keep food on the table or our mansion maintained, but that would be such a boring life.

I wanted to *do* something in the twenty-five years I had.

Brandon seemed ready to move on, clearly unimpressed with our jobs, but Arie was interested, if the glint in his eyes said anything. "You restore classics? My dad had a *Smokey and the Bandit* car. A Pontiac something?"

I smiled, familiar with the film. Like my brothers, I didn't sleep much, so I'd watched pretty much anything that featured a car during the long, dark hours of the night. "A '77 black and gold Pontiac Trans Am. Did it have a screaming chicken on the hood?"

"A what?"

"The giant bird decal. Technically it was supposed to be a firebird, but somewhere along the way it got the 'screaming chicken' nickname."

"Oh yes! It did. He loved that car." Something in Arie's eyes dimmed, but he didn't let it affect his mood. "Ever work on anything like that?"

"Oh, sure. I—"

"Evening, folks. Thanks for joining us tonight." An amplified voice interrupted my answer, and we all turned to the front of the room, where a DJ had been playing music everyone had ignored. A man stood there with the mic, someone we'd chatted with over the course of the evening, but whose name I couldn't remember. "I hope you've had fun catching up with all your friends, but even the best things have to come to an end. This is last call at the bar, and the DJ will be wrapping up in about fifteen minutes. I guess we'll all see each other again in fifteen years, at our twenty-fifth reunion! Cheers." He lifted the beer bottle in his hand at the applause from the crowd.

"We should totally go for dinner while we're in town," Arie announced as the activity around us resumed. "I'd love to hear more about your projects, Drew. And, Josh, if you've got website tips, I'm dying to hear them."

"Really?" Josh seemed stunned at Arie's interest, and not going to lie, I was a little as well.

"Sure! Do you do social media too? I've got an Instagram, but I can never seem to get enough engagement or followers."

"Dinner before we head back to Vancouver sounds great." Brandon grinned.

Honestly, I thought it sounded like something akin to torture. I opened my mouth to politely decline, but Josh spoke up first.

"Sure, we can do that." He looked up at me, and I made sure nothing of my actual thoughts appeared in my expression. "Can't we?"

Behind my smile, my teeth were gritted. "Of course."

"Great!" Arie whipped out his phone. "What's your number? I'll text you so you have mine, and we can make all the arrangements."

Josh and Arie exchanged numbers while Brandon and I looked awkwardly at each other. I wondered if he was as *thrilled* at the idea of dinner as I was. If so, he didn't show it.

Once they finished trading numbers, I clasped Josh's

hand. "If you'll excuse us, I want to get in one dance before we leave. Great meeting you both."

"You too! Can't wait for dinner." Arie was practically bouncing in his excitement, and Brandon tugged him close.

I led Josh onto the dance floor that had finally filled up, now that there was a time limit on the activity. Luckily the song was a slow one, with a standard three-four beat, so I could dance to it. I pulled Josh into my arms and started a waltz.

"Oh," he stammered, looking down at my feet. "You can actually dance."

"Watch me, not my feet." At my instruction, he looked up, nervous but following my lead. "Finnian's wife taught us how. She insisted that every bachelor should know how to dance, because how else would we woo our true loves?"

For an instant, I was back in our brand-new house, Elizabeth in my arms as she laughed at me stepping on her toes yet *again*, with my brothers watching and cheering us on. I blinked the bittersweet memory away, struck again by how much I missed Finnian and her. I was truly happy he'd broken the curse, but it was always bittersweet knowing his immortality had disappeared along with the stone. There was a reason I preferred to focus on the present.

"I wish I could have met her. Finnian too."

"They would have adored you. Like I—we all do."

I did adore him—he was an amazing man, and a huge help to my brothers and me—but somehow stating that so blatantly felt...big. As big as that kiss had been. Rather than dwell on it, I refocused on why I'd instigated our escape from Brandon and Arie.

"Dinner? Are you serious?"

Josh sighed. "I know. I'm sorry. But Arie's so enthusiastic and he seems so genuine. I couldn't say no." His teeth bit into his lower lip for a second. "I can go alone. Tell them you're on a deadline or something. You don't have to come with me."

Like hell I didn't. Letting Josh go by himself was an even worse idea than continuing our charade for another evening. "I'll go."

He brightened. "Yeah?"

"Yeah. But for the record, Brandon is an utter wanker."

That startled a laugh out of him, and the sight of him throwing his head back, his eyes sparkling with humor, hit me like a punch to the gut. I'd done that. I'd made him laugh. It wasn't the first time—we lived together, after all, and I wasn't a stoic bastard like Teague—but again...it felt strangely *big*. Filled with meaning. My stomach fluttered.

"I couldn't agree more," Josh said, merriment dancing in his voice. "But you're not. Thank you, Drew. I...this means a lot."

His laughter faded from his expression as he looked up at me. I met his gaze, hardly realizing I'd stopped moving. People danced around us, but Josh and I were in a bubble, held in a moment of...something. I wanted to kiss him again, even though there was no reason to—no one was paying us any attention. We didn't have an audience. We didn't need to solidify our story.

And yet.

I leaned down, already anticipating the feel of his lips on mine. That jolt of electricity and warmth. He tilted his chin up, a welcome if I'd ever seen one, and closed his eyes.

"Let's make this last dance a fun one!"

I jerked back at the shout from the DJ. The heavy, fast beat pounding out of the speakers shattered the moment between Josh and me. We stared at each other for a second until someone bumped into Josh's back, and I nodded my head toward the door. "Ready to go?"

"I..." The question was there in his eyes, about what we'd almost done.

Don't ask. I don't know what that was.

He must have seen my fervent thoughts on my face, because he gave a slight nod. "Yeah. More than ready."

I hoped we'd be able to leave the weirdness between us on the dance floor.

Chapter 5

Josh

"**H**e *kissed* you?"

I wanted to duck my head and hide my face in my hands, but that was pretty impossible to do when someone was cutting your hair. Unless you wanted to end up with a bald spot. Instead, I grimaced as Em's shriek reverberated throughout the salon, bringing her brother Haider rushing over. Luckily there were no other customers to witness my embarrassment since I was in my typical before-opening time slot.

"Who? Who kissed Josh?" Haider demanded.

"Drew," Em said, waving a hand at Haider to shush him. It didn't work.

He gasped, then held up a stunned fist for me to bump, which I did. "Aw yeah, get it, son."

I couldn't help but smile at their reactions. This was why we were friends—why they insisted I come in before the salon opened, so we could all share a coffee and chat without the distraction of other people. Why I was here for a haircut more often than I truly needed. Not that I needed an excuse to drop by, but hey, I wanted to support them.

To someone walking by and glancing through the windows, they'd seem like an unlikely duo, even though they were siblings. Em's navy blue hair was pulled back in a purposely messy bun, and her black skinny jeans sported artistic tears across the thighs. She wore a loose band T-shirt that was faded from age and use that was large enough to expose one bronze shoulder. Her sharp, glittery nails matched her hair, and she wore no makeup on her amazing sepia skin. She looked like a sparkly punk fairy. In comparison, Haider looked like he'd stepped out of a photo shoot for a school uniform catalogue, but damn, he made the collared, pale yellow shirt with the sleeves rolled up and the pale green sweater vest work with the straight leg, dark wash jeans. Unlike his sister, his bronze skin was highlighted with makeup in all the right places, his dark eyes lined with expertly applied liquid liner.

How I wished I'd known these people in high school. I met Em in college, when she was looking for a guinea pig to practice her stylist skills, and I had a stupid amount of hair that needed to be tamed. Shortly after she graduated, she'd convinced Haider to open a salon with her. She did hair, he did esthetics. They were a great team.

"Why on earth would Drew kiss you?" Em continued. "Not that you aren't eminently cute and kissable, but..."

I fought the blush that threatened to stain my cheeks, but I don't know how successful I was. "Because he was pretending to be my boyfriend."

"Oh my god, I think I need popcorn," Haider trilled. "Dish!"

I laid it all out for them—his proposal to accompany me so I could go to the reunion with a plus-one, the meetup with Brandon and Arie and the kiss we'd shared in their presence, and that moment on the dance floor when I'd been sure he was going to kiss me again. When I'd *wanted* him to kiss me again.

By the time I finished, Em was ready to style my hair, so conversation paused while she wielded the hairdryer and brush. Once she'd shown me the back via a mirror and I'd approved of the finished product, she spun my chair around and flopped into the seat Haider had dragged over for her.

"So what are you going to do?" she demanded.

"Well, um." My teeth found my lower lip for a second. "We're going to dinner with Brandon and Arie tonight."

"With your dickhead ex? Why?"

"Arie's nice. He's the one who asked."

"Where are you going?" Haider asked with a gleam in his eye.

Em smacked his upper arm. "You are *not* going to show up to spy on them, you stalker."

"I'm not sure yet. Brandon and Arie were going to make the reservations." Which likely meant the restaurant's offerings would be stupidly expensive and not at all filling. I rubbed my damp palms on the thighs of my jeans. "I'm trying not to think about it too hard."

Em quirked a brow. "Worried you'll kiss him again?"

"Worried you won't?" Haider countered.

"Yes. No. All of the above?" I sighed.

They didn't know about the curse. Of course they didn't. But that was the only thing I'd been thinking about since we'd gotten home from the reunion last night. From everything the brothers told me about how Finnian instantly knew Elizabeth was his true love, the one who would break the curse, I understood I wasn't that for Drew. He'd known me for almost my entire life—surely he would have clued in before now if I was meant for him, right? So if

I pursued anything with him, it would have to be with the knowledge that in two years, he'd be gone.

I wasn't made for casual flings. I wasn't a friends-with-benefits kind of guy. When I invested myself in a relationship, I was in. If Drew and I tried to date, or hell, simply gave in to the chemistry blooming between us, I was going to end up with my heart broken.

Did I want to take that risk?

Em pushed out of her chair and gave me a hug. "We're here for you, no matter what. You know that, right?"

I gave her a good squeeze. "I know. Thanks."

I ARRIVED home to the sound of raised voices—Rian and Teague. It didn't sound like they were arguing, just overly animated. I tossed my keys in the bowl on the foyer table and followed the curse words emanating from both brothers. They were in the kitchen, in their stone forms, and by their body language alone, I could tell neither was happy.

I paused at the threshold. "What's going on?"

Rian waved a hand at his phone on the counter. None of them could use their phones while in stone form—their fingers were too big and not sensitive enough. It had taken us a few cracked screens early on to figure that out. Now, their phones were protected by a passcode I knew so I could use them as needed on their behalf.

I opened Rian's device to find a series of pictures of the front of his shop, Rune Ink, covered in graffiti. Symbols and words, some of them crude, were scrawled across the glass and brick of the storefront. "What the hell?"

"Right?" He approached to look over my shoulder.

"Look at that. Between the dick and the stars. *Pride.* And over here? That's the rune for cat." Anger all but vibrated through him. "It's got to be that mountain lion shifter Drew ran into the other day. Him or someone in his pride."

I glanced over at Teague. "What do you think?"

He sighed. "I think he's probably right. His wasn't the only business to get tagged lately. It's like they're marking their territory."

"Honestly, I'd rather they piss on the building. Easier to clean up." Rian took the kitchen stool next to Teague. "Can you get someone out to get rid of it, Josh?"

"Of course." I opened a browser tab on my own phone and started searching.

"What are we going to do about them, Teague?"

"I don't know. We can't charge them with anything without proof they were the ones wielding the spray can."

"Which I don't have. The first thing they got was my security camera, from out of frame." He slumped forward, leaning against the counter. "I don't understand why they'd do this, though. They told Drew they'd stay out of our way if we stayed out of theirs, and we're going to be gone altogether in two years. Why antagonize us?"

My eyes flicked to Teague again. He usually tensed at any mention of the remaining two years, because chances were good he didn't have the same time as his brothers. For some reason, he'd woken early this time around. Two years early, in fact. No one knew if the curse's magic was weakening, or if something had interfered with it. But this was Teague's twenty-fifth year awake.

None of us wanted to consider what that might mean.

"To make a point?" I shrugged. "What point that might be, though, I have no idea."

"I couldn't care less if they wanted to settle in Arrington, as long as they keep the peace," Teague said. "Perhaps this is how they usually enter a new territory? I suppose these actions could be seen as intimidation tactics."

They could. But they wouldn't work on the brothers. They'd been around too long and seen and experienced too much to be intimidated by arrogant words and a bit of spray paint.

"I'll look into this Becker who paid Drew a visit," Teague said. "See if I can find out more about why the pride might have chosen Arrington."

"And I'll get someone to clean up that mess." I lifted my phone and gave it a little wiggle. "Already found a company with good ratings."

"Great. Thank you." Rian blew out a breath. "I'm going to see if I can find someone online who might know more than we do."

Teague pressed his lips into a thin line, no easy feat since he was in stone and had lower tusks jutting from his mouth. "That's a waste of time. You think far too much of the internet."

"Maybe," Rian conceded with a one-shoulder shrug. "But it's something I can *do*."

We watched him stalk off in the direction of the stairs.

"He's going to get his heart broken by a network of computers," Teague grumbled before turning his glowing purple eyes to me. "Speaking of broken hearts..."

Oh no. Lecture incoming. "I need to call this company."

"Be careful, all right? You're as much family to me as Drew and Rian are. I don't want you to get hurt with all this *pretending*." His gaze drilled through me, as though he could see into the core of who I was and knew that my heart

43

was dangerously close to getting involved, no matter how hard I fought against it.

Not that I would admit it to him, or anyone.

I pasted on a smile that I hoped looked genuine. "It's all good, Teague. But thanks."

He grunted but didn't call me out on it.

Chapter 6

Drew

D-Day. Date Day. I approached it much like the soldiers who'd stormed the Normandy beaches must have, with a mixture of determination and dread. Not that pretending to be Josh's boyfriend was at all a hardship. But I didn't like the company we were keeping at the beautiful, swanky downtown restaurant Brandon had chosen. Arie was nice enough, and he proved genuine in his interest in my projects and Josh's web knowledge, chatting with us nonstop on everything from how I chose the paint colors for restorations to the social media programs Josh recommended.

Brandon, though? He was, as I'd already determined, a douchebag.

I liked that word.

He didn't have anything to add to the conversation, except to occasionally point out how successful he was. Josh, Arie, and I had barely touched our glasses of wine before Brandon finished his, ordered another bottle, and proceeded to drink all of it. And this was before our appetizers even arrived. It looked like I wasn't going to need the fortification of my new runic tattoo tonight. If he kept going at the same pace, it would be a short night. The drunker he got, the more his eyes strayed to Josh and stayed there until he was all but ignoring his husband. Arie noticed and flagged down a server for some bread and a carafe of water for the table, probably hoping that it would soak up or dilute the wine sloshing around in Brandon's stomach.

"You know, you're cuter than I remember," Brandon announced suddenly.

I paused with my forkful of salad halfway to my mouth, my eyes darting between Josh and Arie.

Josh clearly didn't know what to do with that statement, and neither did Arie. They both looked like they were going to ignore it, which was probably the best course of action. I put the bite in my mouth, focusing on the tang of the salad dressing instead of the secondhand embarrassment rolling through my stomach.

"No, seriously." Brandon hadn't touched his salad, though he'd taken a bite out of a piece of bread—but not nearly enough to counteract the alcohol he'd imbibed. "I dunno what I was thinking, breaking up with you. You're hot, man."

"Brandon," Arie murmured.

I put my fork down. My control on my stone flickered—in retrospect, two nights of maintaining my human skin for an extended period might have been an overenthusiastic prospect, even with the new rune. But I couldn't let Brandon's rudeness slide. "Your husband is sitting right beside you," I reminded him in a low voice. "Show some respect, eh?"

"Psh." Some spittle escaped his mouth with the sound of derision. "Arie doesn't care who I fuck."

I wasn't sure how we'd jumped from inappropriate comments to fucking, but from Arie's expression, it was clear he *did*, in fact, care who his husband fucked. His wide, expressive eyes showed all of his emotions, and right now he was clearly hurt, disappointed, and embarrassed, but not surprised.

It wasn't any of my business what parameters they had —or didn't have—on their relationship, though. All that mattered to me was Josh. And Josh's pale skin was blazing red, his breath coming a little fast. Embarrassment, anger, both?

When he opened his mouth, the source of the flush became clear. Anger, definitely anger. "I forgot how rude you could get after a few drinks," Josh hissed. "I would've hoped you'd grown out of that."

"What, I can't give you a compliment?"

"No, Brandon, you can't." He turned sympathetic eyes to Arie. "I'm sorry, but I think maybe we should go."

As Arie started to nod, Brandon whipped out a hand with surprising accuracy and grabbed Josh's wrist. "No! We haven't even—haven't even eaten yet. Don't be *rude*, Josh," he sneered. "Since that's so fuckin' important to you."

The instant Brandon made contact with Josh, my control wavered. My brothers understood the feeling, but it couldn't be easily explained to anyone else. You had to feel it to truly understand. It felt like a full-body shiver, where my human skin wanted to contract and retreat, making room for the living stone. My core temperature dropped suddenly, leaving me chilled on the inside, while my surroundings were too hot. Under their bindings, my wings flexed, ready to emerge.

I had a few minutes before I lost hold of my human skin, but not many.

"Let him go." I kept my voice low, but there was definitely a subvocal element to it now, a slight reverberation that existed when I spoke in my stone form.

Josh recognized it, and when Brandon didn't release him quickly enough, he jerked his wrist out of his hold in a self-defence move Teague had taught him. It knocked over the jug of water, making us all leap to our feet to avoid getting drenched.

The buzz of conversation and clinks of silverware on plates around us stilled to silence. A waiter rushed forward to help with the spill, and I could feel the eyes of the other diners on me. A quick glance around confirmed that we were indeed the center of attention. Wonderful. So if I lost my hold on my human skin in public for the first time in centuries, I'd have an audience for it. Exactly what this shit-show of a night called for.

Josh pulled out his wallet and dropped five twenties on the table, more than enough to cover our portion of dinner. "Pleasure to meet you, Arie," he said. "Good luck with this one."

"Good *luck*?" Brandon shrieked. "What the fuck am I, a dog? A burden? How the fuck would you even know? I bet Drew's your first boyfriend in years."

I reached for Josh's shoulder and nudged him away from his belligerent ex, guiding him through the maze of tables until we were outside. The crisp October air felt warm on my skin, which was a good indication that I would turn to stone soon.

"Well, I guess we can scratch that place off the list." Josh's voice was a bit shaky, but he confidently took the keys I handed him and got in on the driver's side of my truck without question. Thank whatever gods were out there that I'd gotten a full-size extended cab. I flipped up the seats in the back, crawled in on the floor, laid on my stomach, and debated for a moment if I had time to remove my clothes before I lost my human skin.

Josh got us out of the parking lot and on the road home while I let out a breath and released my hold on my human self. The transformation wasn't painful. Uncomfortable, yes, but not painful. My skin grew tight until I felt like it would split—and suddenly my humanity was gone, replaced by living stone. Although we called this skin stone, it wasn't the same as the form we took on when we slept for a hundred years. Then, we were statues, not living, not capable of any movement. My wings ripped through their binding, plus my shirt and sports jacket, since I was unable to keep them folded tight as I transformed. My pants didn't survive the changed shape of my legs. I kept my head down and mourned my ruined clothes. Even though I had more than enough money to replace them, wasting them like this didn't sit right. I could still remember what it had been like that first time we'd woken with absolutely nothing, having to learn how to sew and patch clothes so they'd fit our non-human bodies. And we'd needed the clothes desperately—that first awakening, we hadn't yet learned how to wear our human skin, so we required cloaks and whatnot for camouflage when we had to venture into a town for supplies.

"You okay?"

Even with the extra-large space, turning to look up at Josh was awkward, so I stayed where I was. "Fine."

"I'm sorry—"

"Don't you dare apologize for him," I growled.

"No, I..." He sighed. "Well, yeah, maybe I was going to. But I should apologize for me. I don't know why I felt we had to spend time with them."

"Arie was nice."

49

"Yeah. I feel kind of sorry about abandoning him to take care of Brandon alone. But not sorry enough to go back and help," he added with a derisive snort. "He married it. He can deal with it."

"True enough." I turned my head to rest on my right cheek, thankful I didn't have any horns that would scratch the interior of my truck. "And as to why you needed to spend time with them? Closure. Pure and simple."

Josh was quiet for a few moments. "Closure," he finally repeated. "I think you're right. I've always wondered what I did wrong. What would have happened if I'd been different? Now...I don't care. I wouldn't take Brandon back if you paid me."

"Good. I'm glad to hear that."

"Also, I'll make a note in my gargoyle caretaker reference guide that two public events in a row with potential douchebags is a *no*."

I barked out a laugh. "See to it that you do."

———

The next day was Sunday, Josh's day off. He usually spent it with his parents, and today was no exception, so Rian and I met Teague for dinner on Josh's orders to make sure he was eating healthy.

He knew Rian and I weren't the best guardians for that, which would be why he made finger quotes every time he said it. The modern era had significant bonuses, like the internet, but oh my god, the *food*. People who grew up in the now truly didn't understand how fortunate they were. I'd never thought there were so many types of food in the world. Thai curry. Vietnamese pho. Sushi. Shawarma. Polish sausage and pierogi. Souvlaki and tzatziki and moussaka. Tacos and burritos. Southern American-style barbeque. The list went on and on. By now, we'd tried pretty much every restaurant in Arrington, and we'd made a few trips to Vancouver to experience the food there—though I wouldn't be rushing back anytime soon. Giant metropolises were *not* one of the bonuses of this era.

Teague, as usual, had chosen where we were going to eat. If he was left to dine on his own, yeah, he usually went for what was easy—coffee, donuts, fast food. But he was probably the foodie-est of us all. Today's restaurant was a tiny Greek place with unbelievable serving sizes and amazing homemade bakery options for dessert. It was always busy, and I didn't understand most of what was being spoken around me, since many of the customers were Greek. It was such a drastic change from the restaurant Brandon and Arie had chosen—loud, with guffaws from the tables around us. The servers were different generations of the same family, going by their similar features, and all of them wore smiles and looked genuinely pleased that we were enjoying the food so much.

"I can't believe he grabbed Josh," Rian said, cutting one of the massive roasted potatoes on his plate into more manageable pieces. "Who even does that?"

"Assholes do," Teague said. "Are they gone?"

I nodded. "They were supposed to leave this morning."

Teague grunted. "So I found some stuff on Becker."

Rian paused as he was dipping his potato in tzatziki. "And?"

"Another asshole. We're surrounded by them." He smirked, and I vaguely recognized the reference to one of the old movies he'd made us watch, with a pair of space heroes who traveled through the stars in a motorhome.

Teague had always been a reticent bastard who

spent way too much time in his own head, but he was even more so this awakening. Waking two years early had affected him greatly, and it had taken a toll on us as well once we'd realized the possible implications. Was the magic failing? Would our time awake and asleep become unpredictable? Or...and I hated to even think this...did it mean that the next time we slept, we wouldn't wake up?

No. I wasn't going to dwell on that. I had two more years, and I wasn't going to waste them worrying about the future.

"We're going to need a little more information than that," Rian prompted, waving his fork.

"They're not an OMG."

I blinked. "An oh my god?"

"Outlaw motorcycle gang," Teague corrected with another smirk. Clearly he'd used that term solely to get a reaction. "Which means they're not involved in organized crime—no drugs, gunrunning, or whatever. At least, not so far as the RCMP know. Which, considering they also don't know they're mountain lion shifters..." He shrugged a shoulder.

"But why are they *here*?"

"Prince George got tired of their shit. The RCMP detachment there raided their gang hangout, going on rumors of drug dealing, but found nothing. A ton of their members were taken in on outstanding warrants, though. Everything from vandalism to assault with a deadly weapon."

"Shit," I breathed.

"Yeah, they might not be a full-on OMG, but they're adjacent, for sure. I don't know why they chose Arrington specifically, but I'm guessing it's because it isn't too far from their old territory and there aren't any other shifter clans in town. Prime real estate for them."

"Except for us."

Teague tipped his head at Rian. "Except for us."

"So, what are we going to do?" I grimaced. "I'm not comfortable with the idea of these guys coming in and making themselves at home, especially once we're asleep."

Judging by the wrinkles in Teague's forehead, the concept didn't work for him, either. "Unless they start breaking the law and leaving proof it's them, there's not much I can do from a legal standpoint."

"It's not always about following the law, brother." Rian leaned over and nudged Teague's shoulder with his own. "Not for things the law doesn't understand."

Teague's frown deepened. "I know. But I'm not prepared to go to war with this pride. Are you?"

I gave Teague's question the consideration it deserved. Was I prepared? We'd never faced anything like this as gargoyles. As men, yes, since you couldn't grow up when we did without participating in a few battles. But as gargoyles, we were usually focused on catching up to where society had progressed, learning new trades, and fitting in—there was no time to pick fights with other supernatural beings. Theoretically, our gargoyle forms could take and dish out significantly more damage than our human ones, but we'd never truly put that to the test. Did I want to spend our last years awake testing that hypothesis?

And regardless of how much damage we could or couldn't take, there was Josh to consider. His parents and family. Perhaps Teague's colleagues. Rian's and my employees. All human, all unaware of the supernatural, except for Josh and his folks, of course. But none of them would be prepared to face a pissed-off shifter. And I *knew* that if we sought to escalate this conflict, Becker and his pride would go after the humans in our lives. Because he was an asshole.

"No," I said at the same time as Rian.

Teague blew out a quiet breath. "Good. I feel the same."

"So what now?" Rian asked. "We let them run all over Arrington?"

The thought made my stone quiver in my gut.

"No, definitely not. Leave it with me. I'll figure something out."

"Hey." I placed my hand on Teague's shoulder. "You know you don't have to do this alone, right?"

He reached up to clasp my hand in his. "I know."

Rian shook his head and scoffed. "You say you know, and then you go and be all big-brother-like, with your 'only I can do this' bullshit."

I quirked a brow at Teague. "He's not wrong, you know."

He patted my hand and picked up his fork again, so I gave his shoulder a squeeze and let go. His shoulders lost some of their stiffness, as though part of him had deflated. That's when I noticed that the skin under his eyes was darker than usual and the creases at the corners more pronounced.

"I do know," he admitted softly. "Let me do some thinking, and we'll come up with a plan in a few days. Acceptable?"

Rian and I shared a look. Teague was conceding the point? Was he sick? The thought emerged as a joking one but quickly turned serious. Wait—*could* he be sick? We hadn't experienced so much as a sniffly nose in all the centuries since we'd been cursed, but maybe the magic was failing in more ways than one.

"Acceptable," Rian agreed.

Pushing down the thoughts of Teague's health, I nodded. "Three days, no more."

Teague held out his hand, palm down, and we piled ours on top. "Three days. And we'll figure out how to protect this town."

Chapter 7

Josh

S undays were for family, and they always had been. Typically, I slept in—the one day I allowed myself to do that—then headed over to my folks' place. They lived on the outskirts of Arrington in a new two-bedroom cottage-like house on the shore of Bobcat Lake. Far enough to have privacy and quiet, close enough that they had all the amenities of the city within a few minutes' drive.

The plan today, Mom announced when I got there, was to go antiquing, do some baking, and then Dad wanted to watch the Canucks game with me. I was all over that. Hockey was awesome. And cookies came from baking, so that was a no-brainer.

Antiquing? Eh, not so much. But Mom loved hunting through the stores, and she needed some muscle with her in case she found a treasure. The dust and old wood made Dad sneeze.

We went to her favorite spot, shockingly called the Antique Barn, which was, in fact, an old barn filled with antiques. There was a particular smell to these places—an astringent scent that I could never place but simply said *old* to my nose. Wood furniture of all sorts was arranged in neat rows, from Victorian pieces that probably had been shipped across the country when the Canadian Pacific Railway was still new to modern items from the 1950s that reminded me of Jane's Diner near the police station. My favorite ones were the art deco servers and chests of drawers. There was something about their design that I liked.

On top of all the furniture, the store had every kind of dish and serving ware you could imagine, in designs as old as 1820, and jewelry and clothes and...everything. Mom had to look through *all* of it because she'd "know what I'm looking for when I find it."

It was going to be a long day.

"Dana! So good to see you." A woman I recognized as the proprietor came bustling over and gave Mom a hug. Where Mom wore jeans, sneakers, a T-shirt with a floral design, and a nice cardigan, this lady was decked out in a flowy dress, brown leather boots, and a matching leather jacket. She turned to me and offered her hand. "Josh, lovely to see you again too."

I felt bad that I couldn't remember her name. "Hi," I said, shaking her hand.

"You must be so proud of Josh for finally snagging one of those O'Reilly boys," the woman said, leaning close to Mom, as though she were sharing a secret.

Which...shit. She kind of was.

Mom blinked. "I'm sorry?"

The woman scoffed. "Josh, you must have told your mother the news!"

"News?" I repeated dumbly, my stomach sinking.

"Yes!" The woman laughed. "The news that you and Drew O'Reilly are dating!"

My gaze went from Mom to the woman and back again. "Um, I... How did you know?"

"I was at Au Claire's last night when you were dealing with that awful man. What a disruption." She wrinkled her nose. "But I heard him say clearly that you and Drew were boyfriends."

Oh no. The truth, no matter how embarrassing, had to come out before this rumor went any further. It was on the tip of my tongue to set the proprietor right, but one look at my mother made me slam my lips shut. She had tears in her eyes. *Tears.* From the woman who didn't even cry at her daughter's wedding.

She swallowed hard. "We'd...we'd hoped..."

They'd hoped? For Drew and me?

She cleared her throat and shook her head. "Josh hadn't shared that news with us yet. But it's amazing."

Oh god. Oh *god.* What did I do now? I should still tell the truth, but the way she was looking at me...as though I'd made all her dreams come true...I couldn't. It was my turn to swallow, but not due to an influx of emotions. Unless you counted a sudden urge to vomit. "Uh. I was...going to?"

Mom, in a very un-Mom-like move, pulled me into a hard hug. Right there. In the middle of the store. I loved my mother, but she was not a public display of affection person with any of her family. We all got hugs at home, maybe a kiss on the cheek, but in public? Nope. That stuff was for private moments. And this was decidedly not one. She hugged me tight enough that I could barely lift my hands to return the embrace.

Awkward.

The proprietor smiled with the satisfaction that her gossip had landed well. "I'll leave you two to browse. Congrats again, Josh. Dana, let me know if you have any questions about anything you find. And say hi to Glenn for me." She swept away with a flounce of her skirt.

Finally, Mom pulled back and surreptitiously wiped her eyes. "I'm so glad."

"Really?"

She caught the note of disbelief in my voice and cocked her head. "Yes, of course. Why? Did you think we wouldn't be?"

"Well, he *is* technically my boss..."

She waved a hand. "They treat you like family more than anything else."

"Not sure if that's more or less awkward than him being my boss." I turned to eye something in one of the glass-doored cabinets to my right, trying to gather the courage to tell her the truth. "Mom—"

"Your dad and I talked about it more than once, you know. When you came out to us. We know the brothers are gay—"

"Rian's pansexual, actually."

She tilted her head in acknowledgment. "Yes, sorry. My point is that your dad and I wondered if maybe you'd connect with one of them someday. Break the curse."

Okay, *whoa.* Hold on. Stop the train, I want to get off. "Mom, I don't think, uh, I'm *that* for Drew."

"Why not?"

"Because..." This whole thing was fake? *Goddammit, grow a pair and tell her, Joshua.* "Because it's, uh, new. And you know the story of how Finnian met Elizabeth. It was instant. It's definitely not that with us."

She positioned herself beside me, looking into the cabinet, and nudged my shoulder with hers. "Maybe that's not the only way. Maybe sometimes it has to build."

"I don't want you to be disappointed if I'm not the one to break the curse for Drew."

"Of course I will be, honey. All three of them deserve to find love, but more so, they deserve to break that awful curse. They've suffered enough." She sighed. "But I'll mostly be disappointed for you because even if you think you're okay with that, it's going to hurt if he goes back to sleep in two years."

"Mom, it's going to hurt, regardless." It was a thought I hadn't allowed myself to fully think and definitely not one I'd said aloud to anyone. But it was completely, one hundred percent true. When the brothers turned back to stone, true stone, I would mourn them. Teague's gruffness that hid a good heart. Rian's unwavering optimism and belief he'd find someone—or something—that could break the curse in a way that didn't require true love. And Drew, with his intent focus on the present, learning the *now*…

Yeah, I was going to miss him the most.

She cupped my cheek and turned my head so I was looking at her. "You're right. It's going to hurt, no matter what. So, honey? Enjoy your time with him to the fullest. If it turns into what we all hope, that would be utterly amazing. But if it doesn't, you'll know you might have eased his burden for a short time. That's worth the pain, don't you think?"

Was it?

WHEN I GOT HOME after the hockey game Dad insisted I watch with him, I found Drew in the garage, despite the late hour. The brothers didn't sleep much on the day-to-day, which wasn't surprising, considering they had hundred-year naps. Drew liked to spend his time tinkering with some of his personal project vehicles, which were so...*dismembered* I couldn't tell what they were supposed to be. This was how he'd excelled so quickly at being a mechanic, these long hours of simply figuring things out.

Tonight, he was hunched over something on the floor of his workspace in the garage, perched on a stool as he examined the whatever-it-was. A hunk of metal, that was all I could tell. The surface of the metal rippled around his thick fingers, his magic influencing its shape and consistency. He was in his stone skin for the moment, wearing only a pair of athletic pants, his wings in a relaxed, folded position. When it came time to do more with the hunk of metal, he'd slip into his human skin, with its more dextrous fingers, but since they could only maintain their human form for so long, I understood why he and his brothers stayed in stone when they could.

He looked up, his blue eyes glowing faintly, even under the shop lights. "How was the game? Did Vancouver win?"

"Four to three," I confirmed. "It went to a shootout."

"Nice." He leaned back, watching my hands, which wouldn't stop wringing themselves together. "What's up?"

Here we go. "Mom found out we're, uh...dating." I made finger quotes as I said the word.

One of his feline brows rose. "And you set her straight?"

"I couldn't. She was so happy, Drew. She had tears in her eyes."

His mouth dropped open, revealing his sharp teeth. "Wait. Your *mom* was almost crying? The woman who didn't cry at her own daughter's wedding?"

That was kind of a legendary thing in our family. "The same."

Jenn Burke

"Shit." He scrubbed a hand over his face, which made a slight grinding sound.

"And then she told Dad, and you know Dad. Waterworks."

"*Shit.*"

"I *couldn't* tell them it was all fake." I paused, gearing up my courage. "But that's not the worst of it."

He leveled his eyes on me, and they were glowing more fiercely now. Out of anger? "What more?"

"They want you and me to come over on Wednesday to watch the next game. As a couple."

"Good god, Josh."

"I know! But they were so happy, Drew."

"Happy to see their baby boy has moved on from a dick like Brandon, no doubt." He cracked a smile.

I shook my head. "Happy for *you*. Hoping we might break the curse. They want that for all of you, desperately. I hadn't realized how strongly they hoped for it."

With a ripple, his stone receded, revealing the human man he truly was. "Can't have this conversation like that," he muttered, shaking his hair out of his eyes. He stood and came closer to me, leaving only a few feet between us. When he looked at me, his now-human eyes were full of compassion his gargoyle eyes couldn't convey. "You know that's not likely, between you and me, right? With Finnian, it was instant recognition."

"I know. And I told them that." My heart sped up. Was I honestly going to do this? Risk this? "But they brought up a very good point."

"And what was that?"

"You deserve some joy. Even if it doesn't...doesn't develop into anything."

Was he closer? He seemed closer. "And what about you?"

I licked my lips, and his eyes immediately caught the movement. Yeah, he was definitely closer than he'd been a moment ago. "I like you. I'm"—oh god, I was going to say it —"attracted to you."

A large, warm hand cupped my cheek. "You need to realize that true love isn't going to come from something that started out as fake."

"I do. I know." I met his eyes steadily. "And...what about you?"

"I can't get our kiss out of my mind," he admitted in a low, rough voice.

"Neither can I," I whispered. "Kiss me again?"

He didn't hesitate, but swept in to join our lips together. I'd braced myself for it not being as good as the other night —maybe some combination of adrenaline and having an audience and the sheer unexpectedness of it had made that particular kiss extraordinary.

I was so wrong.

Drew's lips were supple, warm, a perfect contrast to the scratch of his beard. His tongue gently asked for entry, and I gave it, meeting it eagerly as it dipped inside my mouth to dance with mine. I let out a sound I couldn't identify—a sigh, or maybe a whimper—and Drew pulled me into his arms.

He overwhelmed me in all the best ways. His scent—oil, stone, sweat, metal—enveloped me, surrounding me with his essence. His arms held me close to his chest, and I imagined I could feel his heart pounding against mine. His tongue was demanding now, not asking, and I was okay with that. I'd never felt so consumed as this—as though a kiss would use me up, wring me out—but there was no way I'd protest. It felt too damn good.

Drew pressed me against the wall. My hands skimmed across his abs, finding every ridge, then journeyed upwards, through the hair lightly dashed across his pecs and over his shoulders. Beneath my fingers, his skin flickered.

He pulled back and leaned his forehead against mine. "Sorry," he gasped.

"For what?"

"I can't...holding on to my human skin takes too much concentration, and I can't..."

"Hey. This is me. I like you in either form, okay?"

His eyes met mine. "I can't kiss you when I'm in stone."

Thinking of those sharp teeth of his, I had to agree. "But I can kiss you." Slowly, I let my lips curve into a grin. "And not just on the lips."

His skin wavered again, and suddenly it was the imposing gargoyle staring down at me and not the human. "You mean that?"

If he thought the stone skin, glowing blue eyes, sharp teeth and looming wings would intimidate me, he was about to be reeducated. "Absolutely."

"And no expectations, right? This is for fun."

"No expectations," I agreed. Well, I expected I'd get my heart bruised, if not broken, but that was on me, not him. "What are you waiting for, O'Reilly?"

With a wide grin, he scooped me into his arms and headed into the house.

Chapter 8

Drew

Josh looked amazing in my bed.

I stood at the side of it, watching him all sprawled out, hardly believing this was real. His dark-brown hair was mussed more than usual, and there was a flush to his pale cheeks I usually only saw when he was embarrassed or angry. I hadn't removed his clothes before gently setting him on the bed, so there he lay, in his T-shirt, cardigan, and jeans, toeing off his sneakers so they didn't make a mess of my bedcovers. My eyes were glowing, and his glittered with anticipation, as though there were nowhere else in the world he'd rather be.

It was a heady realization. He wanted this. Wanted *me*. Even as a monster.

"Don't ask me again if I'm sure."

My lips clacked shut, stone on stone. "I wasn't—"

He cut me off with a dismissive sound and sat up to shrug off his sweater and pull off his T-shirt, revealing his lean chest. He didn't have any bulk, but his muscles were defined. His nipples were a dark, ruddy pink, small and flat, begging for a tongue, lips, fingers to make them stand up. There was a cute tuft of hair between his pecs, and more that trailed from his navel below the waistband of his pants. Suddenly I wanted to touch it, to see if it was soft or wiry, to see how he'd react. Would he be ticklish? Would he find it arousing?

I'd forgotten what it was like to have all these questions about a lover.

A lover. It was like the term ambushed me in a dark alley with a club. That was what I was doing here. Taking a lover for the first time in...god, I couldn't even count the years.

"Still with me?" he asked, his voice soft. He'd shifted so he was sitting up.

"Yes. Sorry." I swallowed. "It's...been a long time."

"I bet." He spoke as though he were calming a wild animal, and I suppose he wasn't far off. "If you can't keep your human form when you're being intimate, I imagine you haven't been intimate since..." He trailed off, leaving it open for me to answer. Or not.

But this was Josh. Of course I'd answer. "Near the end of our first twenty-five years awake. We'd discovered we could be human again, only for short periods at first. But then it got easier, and...I needed someone to touch me."

"It didn't work out well?"

"The stable master at the tavern was more than willing to give me a tumble, but as soon as I got excited...this." I waved a hand at my stone form. "We had to run. That's when we made the deal with the wolf pack because we feared the villagers would find us while we slept." We were getting off-topic, further and further away from where I wanted us to be. Hot, heavy, and most importantly, in the present. But could we get back to the mindset we'd been in when we started this downstairs? "Look—"

"You need touch?" Josh's eyes had a twinkle that said we hadn't *quite* lost the plot. He sat on the edge of the bed and waved me forward with both hands. "I can touch you."

The thought of it made whatever blood I had—if I had any in this form, I wasn't sure—heat. "Yes," I hissed, air whistling through my sharp teeth as I obeyed him, moving forward, within his reach. "But I—"

"Let me." He stood and shucked off his jeans, leaving him in briefs that seemed far too small and yet covered too much skin. Sitting again, he grabbed the waistband of my athletic pants and tugged me forward. "Let me give you what you need, Drew."

His fingers slid down my sides, over my hips, pushing down my pants as they went. I could feel it, but barely—my stone form was many things, but sensitive was not one of them.

I must have made some sort of noise because Josh looked up, my pants paused at the point of no return. "Okay?"

"Go harder than you would with—with a human."

He hummed his understanding, then turned his attention back to my pants and what they covered. Determinedly, he tugged them down farther, revealing my nether region. No, wait, that term was too old-fashioned. My dick and balls.

They were larger in this form than my human one, proportionate to my gargoyle bulk, I supposed. If you ignored the fact that my apparatus was made out of living stone, there was nothing odd about it—it was the same shape as any other man's dick. Long, thick, the bulbous head partially exposed by the retracted foreskin. I was half-hard, as I always was in this form—I never got harder or softer. I had no idea how gargoyle physiology worked, even after all these years, but I was capable of orgasm.

Though my own stone hand never felt as good as Josh's firm, silky grip.

"Wow," he murmured, running his hand up and down my length. "You're warm. I mean, I know your skin isn't cold, but it's definitely colder than a human's. But not here."

My head fell back as I soaked in the sensation of being touched. "That feels so good."

"You *are* touch starved, aren't you?" He swiped his other hand across my chest, remembering my instruction, his fingernails scraping across my skin with a pressure that would've left red marks on my human form. "I could keep touching you forever."

I swallowed down a moan. I hadn't expected Josh to take charge in the bedroom, but I wasn't going to complain about it. Feeling his hands all over me, even when he let go of my dick to explore every ridge of stony muscle he could reach, was like ascending to heaven.

Maybe his parents had been on to something. Even if this didn't lead to breaking the curse, having someone's touch for any length of time was so worth it.

"Oh my god." Josh giggled, which brought me back from wherever I'd gone as I reveled in his touch. "Sorry, I'm sorry. But I had a thought."

I couldn't help but smile. "Oh lord. What?"

"You're like a giant cock."

My brows rose. "Excuse me?" I couldn't keep the affronted tone out of my voice.

"Wait, wait, hear me out. You know how a hard cock

feels? A hard human cock. Velvet skin, hard underneath. Right?" His eyes glimmered. "That's you, all over. Your skin's surprisingly supple, but there's this hardness right underneath. Everywhere."

"Great," I said, deadpan. "So I'm a dick."

"Sorry," Josh said through his giggles.

"If I wasn't afraid I'd break the bed and crush you, I'd throw you on it and pin you there until you stopped laughing."

He looked up at me, his eyes sparkling, but with a darker want in them. His grin held both amusement and wickedness, a potent combination. "That would be awesome."

And not possible. In my human form, yes, but that wasn't happening. I wasn't about to dwell on what I didn't have at the moment, not when I had so much available to me right now, more than I'd dreamed of for years. "I thought you could keep touching me forever." I jutted my hips forward in blatant invitation.

The wickedness in his grin increased. His fingers circled my dick again—and then his hot, wet mouth closed over the tip.

"*God.*" The word came out of me in a long, drawn-out prayer. I almost grabbed his head to keep him close but remembered my talons at the last moment. Instead, I clasped my hands behind my back to remove the temptation.

He sucked. Hard, like I'd asked him to. My eyes rolled back and my knees weakened as pleasure shot through me. More pleasure than I'd experienced in centuries. When I'd gotten myself off occasionally over the years, it had been a perfunctory thing, a release, a quick shot of short-lived dopamine to help me get through a particularly bad day. I hadn't even known I could still experience a feeling like this, this warmth and tingling and indescribable *connection*.

Josh took me deeper, his teeth scraping along my stone skin. I wanted to warn him to be careful; not of me, because that felt so good, but of himself. Having to go to the dentist after this amazing blowjob would put a damper on any future activities. And there would be future ones, I had no doubt. Call me selfish, but now that I'd discovered this, discovered him, I wasn't willing to give it up.

Not until I had to.

Focus, Aindréas.

Almost as if he'd sensed my attention had wandered, Josh redoubled his efforts to keep me in the present. He cupped my balls, squeezed, and pulled on them, his grip firm and unwavering. His other hand encircled the base of my dick, stroking in counterpoint to the movement of his mouth. Once again, sensation overwhelmed me, putting my higher brain functions on pause while pleasure rolled through every inch of my body.

"Josh." The gasp was my only warning before I came.

In this time of awakening, I'd discovered novels. They'd been around the last time we awoke in the nineteenth century, even romance novels, but not the explicit and very sexy ones I could find now. And the gay, bi, pan, and lesbian versions of it all, among others. At first I'd been somewhat scandalized that everything was written out in such detail, but then I'd embraced the openness and joy many of them expressed in acts of intimacy between partners. But I'd never thought I would experience the type of sex the authors wrote about.

How wrong I'd been.

Slowly, I came back to myself to find Josh licking his

lips, his briefs pushed down, and his hand working his flushed dick. When he saw me looking at him, he stood. "On the bed," he ordered.

I didn't hesitate. Kicking off my pants, I got onto the bed, opening my wings so they wouldn't be bunched beneath me as I lay on my back. Normally I'd lie on my stomach, but there was no way I was going to miss whatever sight awaited me.

Josh knelt on the bed beside me, staring at me as his hand went back to work. The sight of his cockhead slipping through the circle of his fingers captivated me, as did the slick noise of his skin lubricated by his own precome. "Got lube?"

"I—what? No. I—"

"That's okay. We'll pick some up." He looked down at his hand on his dick, then up at me with a grin. "You like watching me get off?"

My eyes darted to his flushed cheeks and dark, dark gaze. "Yes. I wish I could do it for you."

"We'll practice."

Practice. That meant he wanted to do this again too. *Thank god.*

"Fuck, Drew." He closed his eyes. "I can still taste you on my tongue."

"Yeah?" Arousal stirred within me.

"The feel of you in my mouth, so hard and heavy, I —*fuck.*" He froze, grunting as the first rope of semen spurted out of him to stripe my stomach. The white streak was soon joined by another, and another, and I swept a taloned finger through the warm mess.

He opened his eyes in time to see me flick out my tongue to taste him.

"Christ."

"Now I have your taste on my tongue too." And what a taste. Salty, bitter, sweet—his essence was as overwhelming as all the sensations he'd sparked in me.

Another grunt, another shudder, and a final jet of come. "Drew, you're killing me."

I gathered more of his spend on my finger and licked it off. "Mmm."

He dropped forward with a breathless laugh. Before I could react, he tucked himself against my side, and I automatically wrapped my arm around him. "That was great."

"Yeah?" I was kind of glad I couldn't look him in the face in this position. "I mean, we didn't—uh, go all the way?"

His laughter vibrated through my chest. "We kind of did."

"But there was no..." How many centuries old was I, and I couldn't say it. "You know."

"Penetration?" He levered himself up and, uh-oh, there he was, looking me in the eyes. "Sex doesn't have to equal penetration. Some of the best sex I've had has been simply with mouth and hands. Like what we just did."

Oh, if I were in my human skin, I'd be blushing, no doubt. "What we just did ranked up there for you?"

"Absolutely. Getting you off, knowing no one else has touched you like that in forever?" He settled back down with a sigh. "That definitely rates as one of my best experiences ever, if not *the* best."

That admission warmed me. "It was truly amazing."

"Good. I'm glad." He snuggled closer. "We should get cleaned up."

I could tell by the heaviness of his body against mine that he was loath to move. As was I. "Later. We can cuddle for a bit."

"You like cuddling?"

Truthfully, I hadn't experienced much of it, even before the curse. I'd had no one special in my life, only convenient tumbles where and when I could. But having him curled against me was a sensation I wasn't willing to give up so soon. "I'm finding that with you, I like everything."

"That's because I'm so good." He pressed a kiss to my side, a caress I barely felt physically, but one that shot through my system with the force of a lightning bolt. His breathing evened out shortly thereafter.

I stared at the ceiling, wondering what the hell I'd gotten myself into.

———

A COUPLE OF HOURS LATER, I cracked open my door and slipped into the hall, leaving Josh asleep in my bed. He'd stayed cuddled up against me, dead to the world, and the urge to stay was what pushed me to get up. This was a casual thing. That was it. Of course I liked him, but it wouldn't do to start equating this thing between us with anything like cuddles and intimacy that went beyond the physical.

I turned to head downstairs, only to find Teague leaning against his door, which was across the hall and a few steps down from mine. "Have fun?"

Grimacing, I pushed past him and trotted down the stairs. He followed, clearly unwilling to let me make my—what did they call it? Walk of shame? Whatever the term, my big brother obviously wanted to witness it. Wonderful.

I aimed for the kitchen and he trailed right behind me. "What's going on, Drew?" he asked as I opened the fridge and grabbed a pair of beer cans. We didn't have beverages in glass bottles in the house—they were far too easy to break. At least aluminum cans didn't shatter if we accidentally squeezed them too hard. He accepted the one I tossed to him and settled on a stool at the island, careful to properly distribute the weight of his stone body. We'd gone through several stools before finding ones that were strong enough for us. "Thanks."

Borrowing from his playbook, I grunted, popped the tab on my can, and swallowed a few mouthfuls. I considered not coming clean with him, but that wasn't who we were. We didn't keep things from each other since we were too aware of how little time we had with each other. Too little to keep secrets.

"Josh and I are...trying things out."

One of Teague's pronounced brows rose. "And what exactly does that mean?"

My right wing rose and fell in a shrug. "Right now, it means we're having fun."

"But is he—"

"The one?" I shook my head. "And before you say anything, he knows it. We're on the same page. Neither of us has any expectations."

Teague nodded and sipped his beer. "All right."

I let out a disbelieving chuckle. "What, no brotherly advice? No warnings to be careful?"

"You're not stupid, Drew. I don't need to say any of that. You've already thought it."

"I have."

"Let me say, then, that I hope he makes you happy for however long you have."

It was a vaguely morose wish but a truthful one. Rian was the optimistic one, the dreamer, the one who was constantly searching for a way out, but Teague and I knew we couldn't escape our fate. I lifted my beer, and he tapped his can against it.

"Good luck," he said softly.

You'll need it was the unspoken addendum.

Chapter 9

Josh

Em settled none too gently in the chair across the table from me, her blue hair cascading over her shoulders in a riot of waves. "Okay, spill."

I sipped my macchiato. "Morning."

She scoffed and lifted the lid off her paper cup so she could slurp off the whipped cream topping her cinnamon latte. As always, she picked up a spot of cream on her nose, which I pointed out with a grin. "Shut up," she grumbled, wiping it off. "And quit it with the calm 'morning' shit. You can't text me eggplant emoji and exclamation points at eight on a Monday morning and then greet me all chill like that. But if I ever needed confirmation you got laid..."

My grin widened into a full-on smile.

She smiled back, more excited than grumpy now. "Who? Wait—Drew?"

I bit my lip and nodded. "Drew."

She sat back, stunned. "Holy shit. You're, like, a walking romance trope."

"Huh?"

"Fake boyfriends turning into real boyfriends? Come on, it's a classic."

"Not boyfriends," I corrected her. "Friends with benefits."

Scoffing, she brought her coffee to her lips. "I'm sorry, do you know yourself?"

"What?"

"Josh, hon, every time you've gotten involved with anyone, you've gone all-in in sixty seconds flat."

"I'm not that bad." The protest was weak, because I did, in fact, know myself, but I was trying to ignore that I did.

"You slept with Marco on the first date."

Ugh, Marco. That hadn't been one of my finer decisions. He'd been good-looking and charming...until I'd slept with him twice. I'd been ready to talk about getting serious —I'd discussed it with Em, actually, and hadn't listened to her suggestions to slow down. She'd been right, of course. He ghosted me, and the next time I saw him, it was with a new, starry-eyed moron. Apparently, he had a type.

"Then there was Rocco, who you dated for three weeks. Three weeks that I never saw you, you fell behind in school work, and then he broke up with you because you wouldn't get high with him."

I grimaced. "He wanted me to do meth. Hell no."

"But up to that point, you were all rosy glasses and he could do no wrong."

I sank back into my seat. "I hate that you're right."

She laced her fingers with mine. "Honey, you wear your heart on your sleeve, and that's not a bad thing. But I don't want you to get hurt when he sticks to the friends-with-benefits plan, and you don't."

"I've got my eyes open," I assured her. She didn't know there were parameters for a true relationship with Drew that I'd never meet. Nor did she know that there was a strict time limit on us. In those two ways alone, my arrangement with Drew differed from any other relationship I'd been in. "I'm older. Wiser."

"That's debatable."

"My point is that I know what I'm doing this time."

"Okay. It's your life." She squeezed my fingers. "I'll be here when you need me."

"I know you will."

Suddenly she frowned and made a humming noise.

"What?" I prompted.

"Marco. Rocco. Brando. I'm seeing a pattern."

"Bran*don*." I untwined our fingers and sipped my coffee. "And now Drew. No pattern."

"Maybe that means he'll stick."

We talked some more about the salon and her latest funny customer stories, like the grown man who'd come in with his hair ranging from nearly bald to a few inches in length, with no discernible rhyme or reason to it. Turned out he'd fallen asleep while babysitting his seven-year-old niece, who decided to thank him with a custom haircut. Then we moved on to the newest drama between Haider and his latest boyfriend of the month.

By the time she hugged me in the parking lot and got on her Kawasaki motorcycle, it was well into the afternoon and I was way too caffeinated. But it had been too long since she and I had caught up outside of my usual salon visits. We needed to get together more often like this. Especially if Drew and I were going to keep doing what we were doing. Em would want details and I definitely didn't want to talk about that stuff with Haider present. I loved him, but oh boy. No. It would be all over Arrington's LGBTQ+ scene five minutes after I left.

I pointed my car toward home, on the two-lane highway that led out of town, and ran through the brothers' schedules in my head. Teague wasn't on duty today—he'd started his two-days-off stretch. Rian and Drew had cleared their schedules this morning so the brothers could discuss what to do about Becker and his mountain lions. I wasn't sure what they *could* do. It wasn't like this was the 1800s. They couldn't take the law into their own hands. Could they?

No, with Teague being a cop, he wouldn't let them. I was pretty sure, anyway. Maybe I should look up some good defense lawyers...

The roar of a motorcycle pulled me from my thoughts. At first, I assumed it was Em, chasing me down for some reason. Until I caught sight of three mean-looking Harleys in my mirrors. Two riders wore full helmets, but the third had no protection on his head. My gut jumped. Was this Becker?

No, that made no sense. He didn't know who I was. Unless...he was randomly harassing motorists? It would fit with his asshole actions in Prince George.

Before I could react, the two helmeted riders pulled up on my left, hugging the double yellow line. Becker, or the man I assumed to be Becker, hung back. That uneasy feeling in my gut blossomed into full-out fear. The highway was empty, in that weird space between lunch and rush hour, and we were going about a hundred kilometers per hour. I took my foot off the gas, but Becker banged a fist on the trunk of my Mitsubishi Lancer, startling me into speeding up again.

What the hell did they want?

Suddenly, the front biker on my left swerved into my lane. I jerked the wheel to the right, my heart in my throat. Another pounding on the trunk had me hit the gas again, only to have the second biker on the left swerve this time. Biker One was now in front of me, doing a lazy corkscrew pattern across the full lane so I couldn't pass. Not that I'd try—there was no way my base Lancer could outpace any motorcycle.

My heart pounded. Slamming on the brakes was an option, but I didn't think stopping out here, with no witnesses around, was a good idea. I wasn't sure what they were planning, but it seemed like they wanted to run me off the road. Or maybe simply scare the pants off me. In that case, they'd succeeded.

"Call Teague," I told my phone.

"Okay. Calling Teague O'Reilly on mobile."

He answered after only one ring. "Josh?"

"I've got three bikers harassing me on the highway." As much as I tried to keep my voice from wavering, I couldn't. "One of them matches the description of Becker."

"What are they doing?"

"Trying to—" I cut off with a cry as Biker Two swerved at me again. The right wheels of my car bit into the soil at the side of the highway, and I jerked the wheel to get me back onto the road. The instant I felt the car go sideways and the weight shift, I cursed myself for driving like an inexperienced teenager. I knew better than to overcorrect, but—

Dimly, I heard someone, maybe Drew, call out my name, then the world turned upside down.

Hours later, I sank onto the couch in the living room with a groan of gratitude that I was once again horizontal. True to what the nurses at the hospital said, I was starting to get sore all over. The worst was where the seatbelt had bruised my shoulder and my left elbow, which I'd banged on something when the car rolled. I'd also hit my forehead hard enough to split the skin but not hard enough to cause a concussion, thank god. At least that meant I could come home.

Teague was at the station, sharing what he knew with his colleagues to help them find Becker and his cronies. I wasn't sure what they could be charged with, but Teague was on a bit of a rampage, so I left him to it and wished his fellow cops luck. Rian had veered off to make something for us to eat since it was approaching midnight. None of us had had dinner, and the thought of fast food had made my stomach unhappy.

Drew, though? He was hovering in a way I'd never seen him do before. He was still in his human skin, but it was flickering, going from peachy tan to the gray of his stone and back every few seconds. A scowl had permanently settled onto his face, and he was staring me down as though I'd personally offended him.

I squinted up at him. "You're making my headache worse."

That seemed to knock him out of wherever he'd gone in his head. "Huh?"

"That." I waved a hand at his flickering form. "Pick one."

In an instant, the gargoyle replaced the human. His glowing blue eyes were harsh in the dim light of the living room, but it was better than trying to reconcile skin and stone.

"Thanks." I grunted and closed my eyes.

Then his teeth started grinding.

I opened my eyes again with an exasperated sigh. "Drew."

"They hurt you."

"Technically, I hurt myself with that dumbass move."

He emitted a low growl, one that had ceased to have any effect on me by the age of ten. "Which would never have happened if they hadn't been messing with you."

He wasn't wrong, but I was too tired and sore to argue the point. My eyes fell shut again, heavy enough that it seemed there were weights on my eyelashes. "The cops'll figure it out."

With a grunt that could've been agreement or denial, he seemed to close the topic. "I'll get you some ice."

I was asleep before he got back.

Chapter 10

Drew

This was a stupid move. I *knew* it was, even as I drove around the crappy, sketchy side of Arrington in the middle of the night. Josh was right—Teague and his mates on the force would take care of Becker and the other pride assholes who'd caused Josh's accident. But that logic didn't stop me from trying to hunt them down. Something in me, some instinct, demanded they pay. Now, not later, not through the justice system, which probably wouldn't give them more than a slap on the wrist, anyway.

A text to a long-time customer of mine who owned a less-than-upscale bar pointed me in the direction of a new crowd of bikers who'd recently made themselves a nuisance to the rest of the Arrington fringe community. The cops were likely tracking down similar leads, but I was determined to get to Becker's pride first. What I was going to do when I found him, I...wasn't entirely sure. Punching him in the face sounded like a good start, however.

It didn't take long to find the place my contact told me about. It was a two-story house on a street bookended with self-storage units. It might have been white at some point, but so much of the paint had flaked off and what was left was so dingy, I wasn't sure. A tattered blue tarp covered part of the roof, and the driveway was filled with motorcycles, all in far better shape than the house. A pounding bass beat seeped into the cab of my truck, even with the windows up. Someone lay on the front lawn, which was little more than a few tufts of grass and cracked paving stones; for a moment I wondered if they were dead or unconscious, but then they moved. Passed-out drunk then.

Classy place.

Some figures loitered near the attached garage, behind all the bikes, and they perked up as I pulled my truck to a stop. I opened the door, and the raucous beat coming from the house became even more obnoxious. I wondered why the neighbors hadn't complained. Too intimidated? Or perhaps they'd been invited to the party. After all, this wasn't the type of neighborhood where quiet, family-oriented folks settled down.

One of the guys from the garage intercepted me as I headed for the front door. He was white, balding, with a significant belly, and his skin was sallow and dull. He looked ragged and unhealthy, and far older than I thought shifters could look—assuming he was a shifter. Considering where I was, it was a good guess.

He held up a hand to stop me. "This is private property."

"I'm here to see Becker."

"Becker ain't seeing anyone right now."

I crossed my arms. "He'll see me."

The man puffed up, and his eyes flashed yellow-orange. Definitely a mountain lion shifter then. "Yeah? Or what?"

"Or I'll start kicking ass until he does."

"Yeah, right." He chuckled, glancing over his shoulder at the other guy who'd been with him near the garage.

That's when I struck.

I'd purposely worn an old shirt I wouldn't miss when it was shredded by my wings expanding. I didn't take on my full stone form yet—it wasn't needed. Pieces of my shirt were still falling to the ground when the forearm of my right wing slammed into the side of the guy's neck. He fell sideways, off balance, and I sent him to the ground with another hit to the back of his head. He lay next to the drunk man, equally as motionless.

The other guy was on me quicker than I'd expected. He was in better shape than the first one—not as much of a gut and younger—but one firm flick of my wing sent him flying into the rows of bikes in the driveway. A few of them clattered to the ground, but the music was too loud for it to garner any attention from inside. He didn't get up either.

Excellent.

I aimed for the front door, only for it to pop open when I was a few feet away. A teenager appeared in the gap, zits on his cheeks and all, and his eyes widened as he saw me.

"Get Becker," I ordered.

He nodded and slammed the door shut.

A moment later, the music quieted, and the door flew open again, this time revealing the man I'd come for. He looked much the same as he had when I'd first seen him— dirty-blond hair, slightly greasy, pulled back into a low ponytail, worn leather jacket and combat boots. His rust-colored Henley had a hole near the buttons at his throat. He hesitated for a split second when he saw me, his steps across the house's threshold faltering as he took in the pride members splayed on the ground. Then his lips widened into a smile.

"O'Reilly. To what do we owe the pleasure?"

"You know damn well what," I growled. "Leave us alone."

He leaned casually against one of the pillars holding up the portico as other members of his pride filtered out onto the small porch behind him. I counted at least six, plus the three on the ground outside. God knew how many were still inside the house.

"Seems to me I should be saying that to you." Becker smirked.

"So you're denying you're behind the vandalism? Running our assistant off the road?"

He fake-gasped. "We would *never*."

"Bullshit. We know what happened in Prince George."

"I don't know what you're talking about." He glanced around at his pride. "Anyone? We're law-abiding citizens."

"You're shit disturbers," I shot back. "Last warning, Becker. Leave us alone. Or you'll regret it."

"Hm. That sounds like a threat."

"That's because it is." I turned and started for my truck.

I'd only gone a few steps when I felt something hit my left wing. It thudded to the grass beneath my feet. I paused and bent down to retrieve it. A knife. Its blade was bent from where it had tried to penetrate my stone pinion. If their aim had been better...

I held it up and watched with satisfaction as one of the women next to Becker blanched even paler under the porch lamp. The corners of Becker's eyes were tight with tension, though the smile was still on his lips. As the pride watched, I held the knife in the flat of my palm and concentrated. It took only seconds for the metal to conform to my will, scrunching up into a ball without me moving a muscle. I dropped the ruined weapon to the ground.

"Don't fuck with us."

No one said or did anything as I left.

———

THE GENTLE GLOW of false dawn silvered the horizon when I quietly let myself into the house. The first thing I did was check the couch in the living room. Not seeing Josh there made my heart skip a beat.

"I helped him up to bed," Teague rumbled from the direction of the kitchen. I'd missed seeing him when I came in because I'd been focused on making sure Josh was okay. "Where have you been?"

I thought about not telling him because I knew he'd be pissed, but that wasn't how we worked. "I found Becker."

There was a pause, and then, "*Fuck*, Drew."

I followed Teague as he marched into the kitchen. He banged around in the cupboards, looking for god knew what, as I settled onto a stool at the island and waited for my lecture.

It wasn't long in coming.

"So you arbitrarily decided to escalate this whole thing? Without consulting me, or Rian, or even Josh? He's the one most at risk, you know. And you increased the danger to him without even thinking."

"Oh no, I was thinking," I shot back. "I was thinking that they almost killed him, and that couldn't go unanswered."

"What did you do?"

"Knocked out a couple of their guys." My wing rose in a shrug. "Threatened Becker."

"Íosa Críost." Teague scrubbed a stone hand over his face. "Are you serious?"

"Tadgh, they hurt Josh!" I rarely used Teague's Irish name these days, but sometimes it slipped out.

"Yeah, they did, and it could have been so much worse." He leaned on the counter, his talons scratching against the granite. "And now that you've undermined Becker's authority, I have no doubt he'll retaliate. Then what? Where does it end? You've upped the stakes, Drew, can't you see that?"

His words slammed into me like a punch to the gut. He was right. My intention had been to intimidate Becker into stopping his campaign of harassment. I'd let my anger—and yes, fear—cloud my judgment. Of course, he wouldn't stop simply because I'd shown up at their hangout and threatened him. He needed to save face now.

I braced my elbows on the counter and cradled my face in my hands. "Shite."

"What's got you two hollering at this hour?" Rian stepped into the kitchen, rubbing his eyes, and aimed for the coffee maker.

Teague gestured at me. "Your brother did something stupid."

"Why is he my brother when he does something stupid and not yours?"

As Rian got the coffee going, Teague filled him in on my ill-thought-out escapade. When he was done, Rian simply said, "If you'd have asked, I'd've gone with you."

Teague groaned. "Not you too."

"I'm not saying it was the smartest idea, but I can see where he's coming from, can't you? They hurt Josh."

For some reason, the idea of Rian wanting to retaliate on Josh's behalf didn't sit right with me. It wasn't his job to do so; it was mine. As his...friend. His friend who was sleeping with him. I shook off the weirdly possessive thought.

"I know," Teague said. "They're escalating, and I've still got no idea why. I see only two scenarios if we don't do something. One, they continue to focus on us even after we go to sleep—"

"Which means Josh and perhaps his family would be in danger," I interjected.

"Not to mention us, as statues." Teague's face grew dark as he remembered our youngest brother, Odhrán, who hadn't made it to our second awakening. "The second scenario is they turn their attention to the rest of Arrington once we're gone and try to reestablish themselves in the drug and weapons trade. Unimpeded, at least by any supernatural force."

The coffee maker beeped, and a few moments later, Rian handed out mugs to each of us, doctored the way we preferred. "I don't like either of those scenarios."

"Neither do I," Teague said. "Which is why I've made arrangements for a third."

Something in his voice, his posture, told me I wouldn't like this third option. At all. "What did you do, Teague?"

"I invited the MacGrath pack to come to Arrington."

My coffee mug thudded to the countertop as I stared at Teague in disbelief. "The fuck you did."

My shock was reflected in Rian's widened eyes as well. "How—what?" he said weakly.

"Hear me out. Christopher MacGrath, the young alpha of the pack, contacted me a few years ago. His grandfather, on his deathbed, had asked him to track us down to offer apologies and reparation."

"How the fuck do you offer reparations for abandoning us and allowing our brother to be killed?" I growled.

"It's a stain on their honor, one they're well aware of."

"They didn't seem to be at the time," Rian grumbled.

No, they hadn't, which was one of the reasons we'd fled Ireland for the New World. When we'd confronted them about breaking their promise to watch over us as we slept, the alpha at the time had brushed us off. *He* hadn't made the promise, so therefore it was null and void. He was more interested in bedding the women of his pack and drinking ale than honoring the promise of his forebears.

"From what Christopher said, it's a story that's been passed down through the generations as both a cautionary tale and a reminder that they need to do better. Surprisingly, when I asked him to share what he'd been told, it was very close to the truth. No shining it up for the wolves' sake."

"So you think we can trust them?" I scoffed. "I didn't take you for a sucker."

Teague growled through his tusks. "Give me some credit, will you? I invited them here with some conditions."

"Which they'll break."

"Not this time. Christopher MacGrath has agreed to bind his pack to serve us for a hundred and twenty-seven years until the end of our next awakening period."

"Bind, as in...magically bind?" Rian looked intrigued, probably sifting through all the magic knowledge he'd acquired over the years to determine how it might be done. "And he's okay with that?"

"To restore his pack's honor, yes. He was the one who suggested it."

"Huh."

I crossed my arms. "For the rest of us, what does that mean?"

Rian was the one who spoke up. "It means he's putting his pack in servitude to us. They won't be able to harm us, even when we sleep, and while we're awake, we'll have power over them, much like an alpha does."

"But they already have an alpha."

"Our influence will supersede his."

It was my turn to say *huh*. "This sounds like a big deal."

"Very big," Teague agreed. "They're one of the oldest packs around, with branches in North America and Europe. Christopher's branch emigrated to eastern Canada a hundred years ago or so. They're well-established, with roughly forty members. They'll move out here slowly over the next few months."

I still wasn't convinced this was the best idea, but it would give us allies we didn't currently have. Allies on paper, at least. We'd see if that actually translated to action and if Becker's pride even gave a damn. My money was on *no*.

Which meant Arrington was probably going to get a lot more exciting.

Chapter 11

Josh

My entire body still ached on Wednesday, but not so bad that we couldn't go to Mom and Dad's for the promised hockey night. As soon as we got there, Mom insisted I stretch out on the couch in the upstairs living room. Usually, she made Dad watch his hockey games downstairs in his mancave—not that Dad complained, since that TV was bigger—but they were making an exception tonight. Worked for me. Dad's leather couch wasn't as comfy as this one, with its plush gray fabric and fluffy yellow-starburst throw pillows.

Added to the comfort factor was Drew sitting at the end of the couch, in his human form, with my feet in his lap. I'd expected him to take one of the recliners, but no, he'd settled down on the couch and lifted my feet to rest on his strong thighs, even rubbing them occasionally. Like he needed to keep touching me. He'd been like that since the accident, always hovering nearby, touching me as much as possible. Reassuring himself I was there? It was odd, but I wasn't going to complain.

I didn't miss the worried looks that my parents, my dad

especially, shot my way when they thought I wasn't watching. Dad was clearly concerned about the cut on my forehead, which still had the butterfly bandages on it. The bruise around it had turned a gross shade of purple-green, similar to the other bruises on my torso that were, thankfully, hidden under my sweatshirt.

Finally, he spoke up. "Do you need anything, Josh? Ice? We've got an icepack."

"I'm fine, Dad."

Mom cleared her throat. "It's one of those gel ones. I used it when I sprained my ankle."

"Mom—"

"Did they prescribe any painkillers for you?" Dad asked.

Mom nodded. "Make sure you should take them to stay on top of the pain. It'll help you heal."

"Mom, I'm *fine*."

"You're not fine. Look at you." She jerked to her feet, grabbed my half-empty water glass, and headed for the kitchen. "I'll get you some more water."

Dad watched her leave, then sighed, wiping at his eyes. "She's been worked up ever since you told her about the accident."

She had, huh.

Thank god I hadn't told them the whole truth. As far as they knew, I'd simply drifted off the edge of the road and overcorrected. They had no idea that I'd been *encouraged*, so to speak, by a set of mountain lion bikers intent on worming their way into Arrington. I could well imagine the panic Mom would be in right now if she knew that.

"I understand. But you get that I'm okay, right, Dad? I'm bruised and a bit stiff, but okay."

He sniffled and pulled a tissue from the box next to his

chair. "You're moving and talking, and the rest will heal. That's good enough for me." He shot me a warning look. "But the next time I hear about you not paying attention to the road..."

"I've learned my lesson, don't worry."

I scooted up into a sitting position as Mom returned with my glass and immediately felt the absence of Drew's warmth as my feet left his lap. "Thanks."

She smiled, and it was less tenuous than it had been a few minutes ago. "You're welcome, honey. Let me know if you want that icepack."

"I will, Mom. Thanks."

"Right," she said, clapping her thighs as she sat down. "Let's talk about happier things."

"Or not talk at all and watch the game instead," Dad said, shooting a raised brow at his wife.

"Oh, shush, Glenn. It's not like it's the playoffs or anything." She leaned forward, all eager. "How did you two decide to give dating a go?"

I cast a look at Drew. With all the mayhem, we'd forgotten a very important aspect of preparation for tonight—getting our stories straight. I swallowed, thinking fast, but Drew beat me to the punch.

"You know how sometimes, you see something every day, and it's simple a part of your life. You expect it to be there and don't pay much attention to it. But then, one day, the sunlight hits it a certain way and you stop and go...wow. *That's* a part of my life? How did I get so lucky?" He smiled at me, and I...I melted. His words sounded sincere. Is that what he actually thought? That he was lucky?

Or was he only saying that to make my mom happy?

Well, duh. Of course he was. We were friends with benefits only, and that was okay. He deserved to be touched after going so long without, and I deserved the attention too, after my string of loser boyfriends. But saying *that* to my parents wouldn't fly, and I was glad he understood. I simply needed to remind myself not to buy into it.

"That's so sweet." Mom practically had heart-eyes as she looked at Drew. "I'm happy for you both. It's clear that you truly care for each other."

It was? No, she had to be seeing what she wanted to see.

"Josh already warned me that you're not certain he'll break the curse."

Drew shifted closer to me on the couch, capturing my feet again and lowering them to his lap. As though that's where they belonged. "With Finnian, it was an instant recognition."

"But it might not be the same for all of you." She raised a hand as Drew opened his mouth to argue the point. "All I'm saying is to remain open to the possibilities."

I wanted to tell her that there were no possibilities to be open to, but that would go against everything we were trying to do here. Drew knew I wasn't the one for him—all that was left for us was whatever joy we could find in each other's company, for however long we had.

I was okay with that. I had to be.

I MIGHT BE SORE, but having Drew's hands on me all night made me ache in an entirely different way. When we got home, he started for the garage, but I caught his hand.

"Come to bed with me?" I asked quietly, not because I was embarrassed or unsure, but because I didn't want his brothers to hear and voice their opinion.

He paused, looking down at our joined hands, and I did

the same. It was surprisingly intimate, holding his hand. Such a simple, but meaningful thing. He hadn't abandoned his human form yet—his skin flickered with want, even as his expression held concern.

"You should rest."

"I'm not up for anything athletic, but I could go for slow and easy. How 'bout you?"

The concern on his face was wiped away by a gentle smile. He stepped toward me and tilted my chin up with one callused fingertip, before swooping in for a kiss. I closed my eyes and barely held back a sigh as his tongue swept inside my mouth, slow and easy, as I'd suggested. It was languid, almost, lazy, as though we were lovers of years instead of days. He tasted sweet and a little spicy, thanks to the ginger molasses cookies Mom had plied us with. His usual scent of oil and stone surrounded me like a comforting embrace, mimicking the large, warm hands holding me close while still wary of my sore spots.

After a few moments—or an eternity, I wasn't sure—he pulled back. "Lead the way," he breathed.

I was only too happy to do so.

His bedroom was much the same as I'd left it a few mornings before—mostly neat, with a T-shirt and a pair of athletic pants draped over the chair under the window, and a slightly rumpled emerald green duvet covering the extra-large king sized bed. Though it was muted, the entire room smelled like him, a scent I'd always been aware of but now craved like a crazed dog.

We undressed silently. Drew finished before I did, thanks to my slower, careful movements. I didn't want to aggravate any of my bruises before we got to the good stuff. He'd released his hold on his human form, and the bed protested the weight of his stone skin as he climbed under the covers and held them up for me in invitation. He lay on his side and I slipped into the bed as the little spoon. Which was absolutely perfect.

I sighed as he pulled me close, my back to his chest. His skin, as always, was cooler than mine, but not cold, and it felt good on muscles still recovering from injury. His hand traced the lines of my abs, slowly, almost absently. With anyone else, it would have tickled, but the gentle scratching of his talons gave it enough bite to entice my nerve endings. His half-hard cock poked the top of my thighs, but he didn't seem to be in a rush to do anything with it, as though simply touching me was enough to satisfy him.

Not going to lie, it was working for me in a big way too.

"Thanks," I said.

He nuzzled the back of my neck. "Hm?"

"For not arguing with me about this. For trusting me to know myself."

"You're a grown man." The rumble of his voice vibrated through my back, resonating in my chest. "You can make your own decisions."

"Thanks for that too—for recognizing that I'm not the kid you first met."

He made another *hm* noise in acknowledgment and continued with the nuzzling. "So, what were you thinking?"

Mmm, all the delicious possibilities. "Not anal, not tonight." We'd get there, I had no doubt, but that would be a much more rigorous experience than what I was up for at the moment. Oh, but what could be good... "Grab the lube?" I'd made sure to stock his nightstand with my favorite stuff.

His weight shifted, causing a gap in the coverings that let cold air into our little cocoon. It didn't take long before he was back. "Got it."

"Slick yourself up."

"Thought you didn't want anal." He did as asked, the distinctive sound of lubricated flesh on flesh—or, rather, living stone on living stone—amping up my own arousal.

"Yeah, no, I don't. But this'll be good." I lifted my leg enough to be an obvious invitation. "Slide your cock between my legs."

As soon as I felt the shockingly hot length between my thighs, I squeezed them together.

Drew pulled me close again, his feline-like nose buried in the nape of my neck. "Oh yeah," he groaned as his hips rolled forward.

"Good?"

"So good."

I had to agree. The sensation of him sliding through the tunnel my thighs made, bumping along my taint and nudging my balls—it was almost as good as having him inside me, I had no doubt. He stuck to the program, slow and easy, every movement careful and controlled. Another night, we'd do wild and fast, or rough and hard, but tonight...yeah, this was what I needed.

"You'll like it when I'm inside of you, won't you?" he growled. "I want to watch you ride my dick. Use me for your pleasure. I can picture you sliding up and down, your skin flushed, your pretty red cock bouncing and hitting your stomach, you're going at it so hard."

I gasped at the image he painted. My hand wrapped around my length and squeezed, and my gasp transformed into a moan.

"Like that thought, do you?"

"It's a good one," I said breathlessly.

"I'll lie flat and you can brace your hands on my chest. You can go as hard as you want to. Need to. Slam your ass down until I hit the right spot, over and over again."

"*Fuck*, Drew."

His taloned hand pressed against my lower abdomen, holding me tight as he increased his tempo. Not harder, only faster. "You like me describing it to you?"

"Yes." My hand flew over my cock, twisting at the top how I liked it. "So close."

"Yeah? C'mon then, Josh. Come for me."

And then he scraped his sharp stone teeth over the tendon between my neck and shoulder.

I wasn't sure what it said about me that the hint of danger, the kiss of barely there pain, sent me over the edge, but to be honest, I didn't care. My eyes squeezed shut and my mouth dropped open, but the orgasm was so overwhelming it froze me in place as it overtook everything. Waves and waves of pleasure washed over me. When I'd imagined us in bed together, taking it slow and easy, I'd thought my climax would be a gentle thing, a warm, effortless release that would feel good and help me slide into sleep, but little more.

This was anything but.

As I came down from that amazing high, I was dimly aware of Drew grunting through his orgasm. His semen coated my arm and thighs, and without thought, I scooped some up to help wring out the last aftershocks of my own. He rested his forehead against my shoulder blade and panted.

"Not sure we've got 'slow and easy' down pat," he breathed, ending with something that might have been a chuckle.

I patted the arm that still held me close. "Guess we'll have to keep practicing, then."

Chapter 12

Drew

After that amazing bout of sex, we settled into a comfortable hush. Josh had been quiet so long that I thought he'd fallen asleep. I wasn't tired—content, languid, and eminently comfortable, but not tired. Something about holding him in my arms, still and sated, spoke to a need deep within me. I wasn't sure what it was. Some heretofore unknown desire to offer a safe haven to someone? That was as good an explanation as any.

My drifting thoughts were jerked back to the here-and-now when Josh spoke. "Tell me about the curse?"

Of all the things that could have made good pillow talk, that wasn't one of the topics I would have chosen. "You know about the curse."

"Sure, what's been passed down through the family." He scooted around, hissing a bit as he twinged his bruises, until he faced me. "I've never heard it from the gargoyle's mouth, so to speak."

Careful of my talons, I swept a lock of hair away from his brow. "It's not a fun tale."

"I didn't expect it to be a rom com. Romantic comedy,"

100

he expanded, after seeing my brow furrow. Right, not my favorite genre of movies so I'd forgive myself for missing the reference. "I'll understand if you don't want to talk about it."

I knew he would. But if I were going to share the sordid tale with anyone, it would be Josh. Or any of his predecessors, truly, but none of them had asked. I breathed in, filling my lungs to capacity, and let the air out slowly.

"It was 1523—"

"Wow. I knew it was the sixteenth century, but wow. Oh, sorry, go on."

"It was a totally different world. In some ways, less naive. We were well aware of the things that went bump in the night. Ghosties, goblins, witches, werewolves. Unlike in this modern day, where people rarely believe what their eyes tell them." That had been one of the shocking things about this century: that science and technology had so completely overpowered centuries of innate human knowledge. We'd seen it the last time we'd been awake, but the twenty-first century had taken that ignorance to an extreme level.

"So you believed in stuff like that back then?"

"When we saw evidence of it, how could we not?"

"But, like..." Josh bit his lip. "Were you *sure*? How did you know?"

"Well, being cursed was a good clue." I smiled as Josh chuckled. "But before that, yes, we were sure. We saw the good witches bring farmers' crops back to life or help a mother through a trying birth and survive. We saw the effects of dark magic too. We heard the werewolves howl on the full moon—"

"There were wolves in Ireland in the 1500s, weren't there? Could have been non-shifter wolves."

"You've clearly never heard a werewolf's howl. The sound is indescribable—filled with magic and chilling to your bones."

"Oh."

"At any rate, the point is that we *knew*. We lived with magic every day. Some overt, some subtle, some inherent. But it was always there. Perhaps we were more attuned to it because our grandmother had been gifted with some magic. Not enough to be called a witch, but enough to understand the weather, to brew healing potions and tonics, and whatnot. She told us that we had witches further back in our ancestry, and our great-aunt Líadan had a significant amount of power. She had no interest in herbs and tonics, so most people didn't realize her abilities."

"So you had magic in your blood even before the curse? That's cool."

"We did. I suppose the curse, or perhaps our great-aunt's tinkering with it, brought out our talents."

"Huh?"

"I'll get there." I smiled sadly. "Our uncle was Eoghan Ruadh, the king of Breifne O'Reilly—"

"Wait. Wait, wait, wait." Josh levered himself up onto one elbow. "I knew you were something like nobility, but are you saying you were fucking *royalty*?"

"Didn't know you were sleeping with a prince, did you?" I chuckled. "No, it didn't work like that. It was an elective monarchy, not a hereditary one. Think of it like being second cousins once removed or some such to a billionaire. You're part of the family, and you might get some benefit and prestige from that, but generally you're on your own in the world."

"Okay. That's...a bit reassuring, actually."

We were getting into the darker part of the story, and

my smile faded. "My grandmother had passed that winter, and Mam went to a new herbalist in the area that summer for a tonic to ease the pain in Da's joints and one to help her headaches. Instead, the woman sold my mother poison. Da died first since he needed more of his tonic, but Mam had no idea her tonic was poisoned as well. She fell ill with her first small dose and lingered a few more days."

"My god, Drew. That's...that's terrible. I'm so sorry."

I ducked my head because even all these years later, remembering Da's still, still form and Mam's low, unending moans of pain made my heart ache as though that herbalist had skewered it. "Thank you," I managed after a moment. "Eoghan Ruadh, my da's brother, confronted the woman and demanded she pay us a fine, per Brehon law—the law of early Ireland. But she defied him, and so my uncle gave her to us. We could await payment, which was never going to happen, sell her into slavery, or kill her. We opted for the latter."

"Drew." Josh's voice was all but strangled and tears welled in his eyes. "That..."

"Horrible, I know, but it was our right. Except as Teague lifted his sword to run her through, with our kin at our backs to witness it, she cursed the five of us. We turned to stone right there."

"But *why*? Why was she so focused on doing your family so much harm?"

"I don't know. When we awoke a hundred years later, it was to find our kingdom and family gone. We'd been moved to a church that had been new the last time we'd seen it, but was falling apart by then. The priest who lived there was old and nearly blind, but had been told what to share with us when—if—we woke. At the moment of our curse, Líadan, our great-aunt, counteracted as much of the spell as she could, limiting our time in stone to stretches of one hundred years, followed by a quarter-century awake. She's the reason we have hope at all that we might break the curse with true love. The priest said she was angry that she couldn't do more for us, but, I've thanked her in my prayers multiple times for what she accomplished."

"I'd always wondered why the curse had those loopholes." Josh had settled back down, cuddling close to me.

"He also told us that the woman who killed my parents escaped in the panic after we turned to stone."

He jerked back, wincing at the quick movement. "She was never punished?"

"Not as far as I know. She destroyed my family for no known reason, and got away with it."

"Oh my god, Drew." The horror in his voice said it all. "I... I don't know what to say."

I sighed and pulled him close. "It's been five hundred years, and I don't know either."

TALKING about my past always dropped me into a dark mood. Perhaps I should have put off Josh's request until after we'd met with the MacGrath pack, but I didn't see how I could have. He'd been so gently earnest, and it had felt like the right time to share.

Now I'd have to deal with the consequences. Specifically feeling somewhat fragile as we approached Christopher MacGrath and three other wolves at a rest area on the highway, close to where Josh had been run off the road.

Another thing to darken my mood.

Christopher MacGrath was more rugged than I'd expected, as though he were used to daily hard labor. He was white, with short, messy medium-brown hair, but I didn't think it was styled that way on purpose. He had a close-cropped, full beard that crept down his throat, almost to the tuft of hair visible at the apex of the V-neck of his gray tee. Over the T-shirt, he wore an open long-sleeved flannel button-down, but the width of his biceps and forearms was still clear enough. His hefty thighs challenged his jeans as well.

The most captivating thing about him, though, was his crystal-clear amber eyes, the mark of an alpha wolf.

"Wow," Josh breathed from the back seat.

The slight reverence in his voice did not help my mood at all.

MacGrath's lips were curved in a welcoming, closed-mouth smile as Rian, Teague, Josh and I got out of my truck. Right, no baring of teeth in werewolf culture. At our approach, he gave us a cordial nod. "Good morning." The two men and one woman with him mirrored his nod but said nothing. Unlike their alpha, they had normal-colored human eyes—brown, green, and hazel.

"Good morning," Teague replied. We all wore our human skin, in case someone not involved with this meeting came by. It had been Teague who'd insisted on the location —not busy, but not isolated either, and neutral to both us and the pack. It was all a carefully orchestrated display of trust on our part. On the wolves' part too, Teague had insisted, but I wasn't sure I was ready to believe that.

I glanced behind me to ensure Josh was staying at the rear, as we'd agreed. His being here wasn't ideal, but he'd insisted, arguing that since he was going to be the one to maintain the relationship with the wolves in a couple of years, he should be involved from the start. He wasn't wrong, but that did little to calm me. The urge to spread

Jenn Burke

my wings so the wolves couldn't see him was nigh irresistible.

"Christopher MacGrath." He waved to his companions. "Milo, Gage, and Olivia."

"I'm Teague O'Reilly, and these are my brothers, Drew and Rian, and our assistant and guardian, Josh Pallesen."

MacGrath's nose twitched. "He's human."

"Got a problem with that?" I growled.

He lifted a hand in supplication. "No. I was surprised you'd choose a human as a guardian, that's all."

"It's a long story," Josh said.

The wolves' gazes focused on Josh as he spoke, and the hair at the base of my neck tingled. I did not appreciate them watching him so intently. Shifting slightly to the side, I blocked their line of sight.

Rian stepped up next to Teague. "This isn't all of your pack?"

"No, only the few who have moved out here with me for the moment. Once we've finalized the purchase of your property—"

"Property? Wait—the ranch?" Josh broke in, then pushed me aside so he could confront Teague.

"Yes, this is why I bought the ranch."

I frowned. "You were planning this? Even before the cats?"

"Even before."

I'd wondered why Teague had bought the expansive property ten years ago. At the time, I thought it was simply an investment. I should have known he was thinking long term; he always was. That said, I didn't know if I was glad inviting the wolves here wasn't an impulsive decision.

MacGrath cleared his throat. "Having four thousand private acres to run in is a dream come true."

106

"I'm not interested in your opinion," I growled at him.

His amber eyes glinted at my tone, though they didn't quite glow as ours did when we were in our stone skins. "I apologize."

"No, it's Drew who should apologize," Teague said sharply. "My brothers are having difficulty getting past our unfortunate history with your pack."

It was MacGrath's turn to dip his head. "I understand. It's unrealistic for you to trust us simply because we asked. It's my hope that we can repair the relationship between our pack and your family."

"That remains to be seen." I took a few steps toward MacGrath. His pack members drew closer to their alpha at my approach, their shoulders growing tight. For his part, MacGrath didn't move. "Our youngest brother died because your pack broke its oath."

"I know." There was something in his eyes. Remorse, or regret, perhaps.

I ignored it. "You *don't* know. You can't know what it's like to awaken from your curse to find a pile of dust and rubble where your brother had been—"

"Drew—"

MacGrath glanced over my shoulder at Teague's attempt to interrupt. "It's fine. He's right. I can't know what that's like." His gaze slid back to mine. "But I promise you'll never experience that again."

"Your word means nothing."

"So let us prove it to you."

Our eyes met and held. Neither of us looked away. I wasn't sure I would have, but Josh's quiet "Drew" spurred me to take a different action. I nodded and held out my hand.

"Welcome to Arrington."

Chapter 13

Josh

A day after meeting the wolves for the first time, they were in the gargoyles' territory for the binding ritual.

The brothers were on edge, even Teague. The binding ritual couldn't be done elsewhere, since there was too great of a chance it would be interrupted, but the mansion was their sanctuary, and only a few people were invited to darken its doors. Well, me and my parents. My siblings too, when they were in town. And that was it. To have what were essentially strangers on the back patio was clearly not something they were comfortable with. Teague was even less verbal than usual, but his tail was swishing back and forth, giving away his agitation. Rian was yawning a lot, and I knew it couldn't be because he was tired, so it had to be stress-induced. And Drew was walking around with a permanent scowl etched into his stone features, baring his shark-like teeth at any provocation, no matter how minor.

Like me asking if he could bring a tray with a coffee carafe and cups out to our guests.

"I'm not a servant," he growled.

"No, you're supposed to be a gracious host. You're not doing a very good impression of one so far."

He glanced through the glass patio doors to watch Christopher MacGrath speak with Teague. We had the fire tables lit, and Christopher had assured me the wolves weren't affected by the minor chill in the air, preferring to be outside rather than inside. He wore the same type of outfit he'd had on yesterday—a flannel over a T-shirt and worn jeans. He'd fit right in as a lumberjack.

My eyes traced over his *very* nice form before returning to Drew, who was scowling even harder. "What?"

"Why are you looking at him like that?"

"Like what?"

"You're about to drool."

I resisted the urge to run a hand over my mouth to verify I hadn't, in fact, drooled. "He's very pretty."

A low rumble emanated from Drew's chest. "*Pretty* isn't the word I'd use."

"No? How'd you describe him, then?"

"Annoying. Arrogant. Cocky. Annoying."

"You said that already." I chuckled at his ridiculousness. "You need to give him a chance."

"Is that what you're going to do? Give him a chance when I'm—" He broke off, grabbed the tray from my hands, and marched outside.

I stared after him, sure my confusion was written all over my face. Did he think I *wanted* Christopher? I mean, he was nice to look at, and I definitely wasn't dead. But I didn't want him. Not like I wanted Drew.

I needed to reassure him, but maybe doing that in the middle of a pack of werewolves was not the time. It could wait until this ritual was done. Later, when we were alone, I would make it very clear who was on my radar...and it definitely wasn't Christopher MacGrath.

In the intervening day since we'd first met with the wolves, their speaker had arrived. At first I'd thought that, from the title, they were supposed to be a mediator or something, but it seemed they were more of a spiritual guide. Similar to a shaman, maybe, with the name of Moon Speaker. They wore furs—what type, I couldn't tell—and leather, and their long, graying hair was separated into random tails and wrapped with leather and beads that glistened white in the patio lights. They carried a staff topped with a metallic crescent moon, tips pointing up, with crystals bound by wire and leather at random spots along the length of it.

I understood that they would be conducting the ritual to bind the wolves to the gargoyles. The speaker exuded a dichotomy of energies—calm and serene, but also wild and chaotic. It simultaneously encouraged me to relax and run for my life because I was in the presence of a predator.

I was perfectly fine with them being on the other side of the patio, thank you very much.

I hung back as the speaker gestured the wolves and gargoyles forward, to join them on the mostly brown grass. In addition to Christopher and the speaker, there were five other representatives from his pack—his three enforcers and the dame, who apparently looked after the pups or cubs or... hell, maybe they called them kids. Anyway. The last member was an elderly male, still strong and spry. If he didn't have hair as white as the driven snow, I would've guessed him to be in his fifties when it was more likely he was in his seventies. The wolves arranged themselves to the right of the speaker, and Drew and his brothers stood to their left, facing the pack.

"Joshua."

Though I hadn't heard them speak, it was clear whose voice that was. Low and rough, it was impossible to peg it as male or female. Somehow, I wasn't surprised that the speaker knew my name. They probably knew the brothers' Irish names too, something I always had a rough time remembering.

I gripped the back of the chair I was standing behind a bit tighter. "Yes?"

"You are a member of the gargoyles' clan, are you not?"

"Uh, I...yes?" I looked to Teague for confirmation, but it was Drew's emphatic nod that caught my eye. "Yes. I am."

"Then stand with your family."

"Oh, uh, okay." I booted it across the lawn to stand beside Drew, resisting the entirely inappropriate urge to hold his hand. We weren't on a date, for god's sake. Since when was I a hand-holding kind of guy? And since when was what Drew and I doing with each other *dating*?

Yeah, no, not dating. We were enjoying each other's company.

The speaker nodded in approval as I settled in beside Drew, then shifted their staff so it was positioned before them. It divided their face into two equal halves, both still unerringly androgynous. "Beneath Grandmother Moon, we stand before each other with openness and hope in our hearts, knowing she and her sisters, Mother and Maiden Moon, see and know all that we hold deep inside. Grandmother Moon bears witness to the oaths that will be said here today. She will judge them and find them worthy or unworthy, and bless them or not.

"The history between our two clans has been fraught. It is through no fault of anyone at this gathering, and yet the responsibility lay upon the shoulders of the Alpha

MacGrath. Christopher Shaughnessy MacGrath, state the malfeasance visited upon the brothers Ó Raghailligh by your pack."

My brows rose at the perfect pronunciation of the brothers' Irish name. Damn, could I call it, or what?

Christopher stepped forward until he was right in front of the speaker, facing Teague, who stood between his two brothers. The alpha wolf kept his head bowed, a sign of submission.

"In the year 1645, my ancestor, Cathoir MacGrath, then Alpha MacGrath, pledged to the brothers O'Reilly to watch over them as they slept in return for their help in repairing a rift with a rival pack and in establishing a trade relationship with a nearby town. It was an agreement witnessed by his mate, his second-in-command, and his enforcers, all of whom had been in favor of the arrangement. The brothers fulfilled their end of the agreement, using their diplomatic skills and their prowess in negotiation, and trusted that we would hold up our commitment once they slept.

"However, ten years after they turned to stone, Cathoir MacGrath's son, Einrí, killed his father in order to take control of the pack. His greed and gluttony led to a dark time in our pack's history. Eighty-five years later, Einrí's corrupt grandson and two of his pack mates stole into the compound where the gargoyles slept and pushed one of the stone figures to the ground."

My gaze darted to the gargoyles. From what Drew had told me, they'd suspected the wolves had been behind the murder of Odhrán, their youngest brother, but until now, they hadn't *known*. Drew had his fists clenched at his sides, Rian's eyes were wide and disbelieving, and Teague looked as stoic as ever, but there was tension vibrating along his jaw.

I moved closer to Drew and brushed my hand down his inner forearm, encouraging him to open his hand. When he did, I slipped my fingers between his. Screw what anyone else thought—he needed to know I was here and supported him. Through whatever else Christopher had to reveal.

"The statue shattered into dust and rubble and, according to the tales passed down, let out a ghostly scream of pain that faded into the night. It was that scream that saved the other brothers, as it frightened the pups so much they fled."

The sound of stone grinding on stone caught my attention, and I dug my fingernails into Drew's knuckles, hard enough he could feel it. Out of the corner of my eye, I saw him unclench his jaw.

"When the brothers awoke and found their youngest sibling murdered, they rightfully approached my pack to find out why we hadn't protected them. The Alpha MacGrath at the time, Fearghas MacGrath, was much like his father, Einrí, and further compounded our shame by not revealing who was responsible for their brother's death and refusing to honor his debt to the O'Reillys. The brothers were run off pack lands." Christopher surprised me—surprised all of us—by sinking to his knees. "My pack owes you a debt of honor we cannot pay. You may ask of us what you wish in recompense that should have been yours nearly three hundred years ago."

"What say you, brothers Ó Raghailligh?" the speaker said, turning to Teague. Christopher remained motionless on the ground. "The MacGrath pack caused the death of one of your own and harmed the rest of you through the refusal of the support we'd promised. Our tradition and the law of your homeland states that you may request payment in monetary form or in blood. Or you may wish to have the pack pay via subservience."

Payment in blood? I hadn't realized that option was on the table, but I couldn't see the brothers taking it even if they hadn't already worked out the pack's payment. As angry as Drew was at the wolves, for instance, I knew he wouldn't truly take any physical vengeance on the pack members standing before us...or any of them. They weren't their great-great-times-whatever grandfathers. They wanted to make this right.

"The MacGrath pack will pay in subservience to our family the time they had pledged to protect us, plus the two years before we sleep, and an additional twenty-five years once we awaken," Teague intoned.

"Alpha MacGrath?"

Christopher didn't lift his head. "We agree."

"For the next one hundred and twenty-seven years, your pack will be in service to the Ó Raghailligh family, the members of whom stand before you now, and any future members that join them."

My brows twitched at the strange statement. The family wasn't going to expand.

"We agree," Christopher said again.

"Every member of your pack will look to them as though they are alphas."

"We agree."

"Their power will supersede even your own, meaning you will answer to them as well."

If I'd expected any hesitation to that statement, I didn't hear any. Christopher immediately said, "We agree."

The speaker nodded and gestured with one hand.

"Tadgh Ó Raghailligh, as the head of your family, please step forward."

Teague did so, moving until he stood directly before Christopher. The speaker joined them and took one of Teague's hands into their own, placing it atop Christopher's bowed head.

"As witnessed today by Grandmother Moon, by the representatives of the MacGrath pack, and by the Ó Raghailligh family, I hereby bind the MacGrath pack to the will of the Ó Raghailligh family for one hundred and twenty-seven years. After that time, the debt owed shall be considered paid in full." They tapped the butt of their staff on the lawn, and I swear I saw something flicker along its length—something that raced from the speaker's hand into Teague's and down through Christopher's skull.

"It is so," the speaker said, then stepped back. "You may—"

A gunshot echoed across our property. The speaker stared down at a crimson stain quickly spreading across the white pelt on their right shoulder and, a second later, crumpled.

"Everybody down!" Teague shouted, hitting the dirt. He took Rian with him. Though the brothers couldn't be hurt by regular bullets, armor piercing or hollowpoints could do a lot of damage, and standard bullets could ricochet off their stone to hit others.

I didn't have a chance to obey Teague's order. Drew tackled me, knocking the wind out of me. I could barely register his heavy stone body shielding me as I gasped for air that wouldn't come. Vaguely, I heard more shots whistle by, striking the dirt with muted thuds, and another cry of pain. Then there was a terrible growl, so menacing it cut through the fog of my struggles, followed by a howl in a different timbre. Drew had been right—a werewolf's howl was nothing like a normal wolf's.

"To the west," Teague said.

I could only surmise that a pair of the wolves had shifted to chase down the shooter. Shooters? I had no idea. Seconds later, a fierce feline roar cut through the night. Well, that left no doubt who was behind this attack. If we'd ever wondered.

I patted Drew's biceps. My ability to draw in air was back, but I couldn't breathe with his weight pressing me into the ground. He levered himself up to look at me, his glowing blue eyes unreadable, but the lines of his face telegraphing his concern.

"Josh? Are you hit?"

"Can't...breathe."

"Oh my god. Where? Where are you hit?" He pulled back even farther and ran his hands along my side.

With the additional space, I could finally suck in a full breath, which I did, noisily. "I'm not hit. But you're *heavy*."

It took him a second to absorb what I said. Then some of the tension in his face eased. "Oh. Sorry."

He started to roll away entirely, but I stopped him. "Don't apologize. You protected me."

"Always. I...always," he said more softly. We shared a look I couldn't categorize, and then he got up to check on the others.

I remained on the ground, wondering what the hell I was feeling.

Chapter 14

Drew

I had never been so filled with the urge to rip, rend, maim, even kill. My eyes were blazing as hard as I'd ever felt them glow, and my hands kept flexing into fists without my consent, my talons biting into my palms. I couldn't stand still, instead walking from the living room to the kitchen, then the dining room and back.

Those cat bastards had come onto *our* property. Shot two of *our* guests. Endangered my family. Endangered *Josh*.

That last thought threatened to push me out the door to confront Becker again. And this time, it wouldn't be with words.

Rian laid a hand on my shoulder, stopping me at the threshold of the dining room, where everyone was gathered. "Hey. You're going to wear a rut in the floor."

The dining room, a room that normally felt three sizes too big for Rian, Teague, Josh, and me, seemed far too small with the addition of the wolves. The speaker was sitting in one of the chairs, their wound far less severe than it had appeared to be outside. Or perhaps that was the werewolf

117

healing at work. One of MacGrath's enforcers, Gage, had been winged, a wound that had already closed and looked a week old.

Josh was puttering around, neatly weaving out of my way whenever my pacing brought us in reach of each other, refreshing drinks and making sure the trays of sandwiches and finger foods we'd been going to serve outside were arranged nicely on the buffet. He hadn't stopped since he'd gotten himself off the ground and brushed the dirt from his clothes. I wondered if he was using the activity to keep himself from thinking about what might have been.

The same way I was using my pacing and anger to shield myself. Underneath was an emotion I wasn't ready to explore, especially not in the company of our new allies.

"Príomha, should we plan a retaliation?" MacGrath had taken to calling Teague the Irish equivalent of *prime*, I supposed in recognition of his new standing in the pack. His pronunciation wasn't bad. A little too hard on the long *i* and not soft enough on the vuh sound of the *mh*, but not bad.

Teague braced his hands on the edge of the table and shook his head. "I don't want to start an all-out war. We need to plan for our long-term goal of ousting them from Arrington."

"So we're going to let them get away with shooting us?" Gage slammed a hand on the table. "That's bullshit."

"Settle," MacGrath ordered.

After a growl of protest, Gage slumped back into his seat.

MacGrath turned his attention back to Teague. "With all due respect, I agree with Gage. To some extent. If we let this go unanswered, the pride will see us as weak."

"It's not going to go unanswered, I can assure you of that," Teague rumbled. "But we need to be smart about it. If this escalates more than it already has, we'll start drawing the attention of the human authorities, or innocents will be hurt. Either way, we can't let that happen."

Humans were blissfully unaware of the supernatural world, and that's how every supernatural creature I'd ever met wanted it to stay. It wasn't like it was when we'd been cursed; as I'd told Josh, back then, everyone was well aware of the things that went bump in the night. That awareness had dimmed over the countless generations between now and then, leaving behind only legends and fairytales. Humans were eager to go to war over each other's religions; I could only imagine what they'd do if they discovered different species dwelling among them. And the thought of being taken to some clandestine lab to be experimented on... no. No, thank you. Sometimes science wasn't a blessing.

"I have an idea." MacGrath's other male enforcer, Milo, stepped forward from where he'd been leaning against the wall. "With your permission, Alpha. And, uh, Príomha."

Teague nodded, and MacGrath gestured for the enforcer to approach the table. "Go ahead."

Milo looked younger than the other enforcers, maybe mid-twenties instead of in his thirties. His dark-blond hair was pulled into a messy bun, as though he'd forgone a comb and simply used his fingers to pull it back and style it. His eyes were deep brown, and he sported stubble that matched the darker roots of his hair. He came up to the table and bowed his head.

"I agree with Príomha, that any sort of physical retaliation will escalate the conflict out of our control."

"It's not in our control now," Gage grumbled. Olivia

smacked the back of his head. He opened his mouth to cuss her out, given the expression on his face, but a low growl from MacGrath stopped that behavior in its tracks.

Milo shot Gage a dirty look and continued. "But we can force them out of Arrington in another way."

"And what does that mean?" Teague asked.

"They're handling things like their beasts would—physical intimidation, attacking, striking, and so on. What we need to do is think with our human brains and, like you said, be *smart* about how we retaliate. We do it with computers."

"Explain," MacGrath said.

"Hacking. If we can get the right info, we can drain their bank accounts, freeze their utilities, convince any of their lenders to call in their loans or repossess their bikes... the possibilities are endless."

Teague was already shaking his head before Milo finished. "Even if our names aren't plastered all over these activities—which are illegal, by the way, and you might remember I'm a cop." He raised a brow, and Milo looked abashed for a second, as though he *had* forgotten—or perhaps he hadn't known. "At any rate, even if these things would be carried out anonymously, Becker would figure out soon enough that we're behind it all."

"Agreed. That's where the rest of my plan comes in. If we were to do all of this without an endgame in mind, it could and would spiral. But here's what I'm thinking. We incapacitate them online, then offer the only solution: they leave Arrington permanently, and we'll give them their lives back."

"Like ransomware," Josh said from his spot in the doorway.

Milo pointed a finger at him. "Exactly. And yes, it's

technically illegal, but unless you can think of a *legal* way to get them out of our hair..."

Teague grimaced. "Point taken. Drew, Rian, Christopher, Josh? What do you think?"

"I'm behind whatever works to get them out of our city," I said. Even if I'd prefer the physical retaliation approach, logically I knew Teague and Milo were right. Doing it this way would hurt them more—hopefully—and encourage them to get out. "But are we sure this will work like you think it will? And can you actually do it? If we don't paralyze them completely, there's a good chance they'll come after us, because as Teague said, they'll know who's responsible. I don't want my—Jo—anyone to be hurt again."

Rian shot me a wicked grin, likely knowing exactly why I'd tripped over my tongue there. Josh *wasn't* my boyfriend, so I wasn't sure why that title had almost fallen from my lips. He also wasn't mine by any means. I wasn't sure where this possessiveness was coming from, first when he'd been watching MacGrath and now with the urge to tear Becker to shreds for even coming close to hurting him. Again I would never win awards for patience or self-restraint, but this went above and beyond my usual living in the now mantra.

"Milo's got the skills to pull it off, though you're right—we'll need to be quick and careful about it," MacGrath said. "We can go through their trash and tail them, and Milo can see what he can dig up online."

"Right," Milo said. "And when we have a good amount of usable intel, we can strike. All the things at once. That way, they won't have room to breathe. Then we offer to meet with Becker and give him an out."

I wasn't convinced "all the things at once" was going to happen, or that it would be enough to make Becker desperate enough to want to get out. But I didn't have any other options to offer, despite my instincts urging me to grab Josh and stuff him in a safe house somewhere. Not that we had one. If it would keep him safe, though, I'd buy one.

Perhaps that wasn't such a bad idea.

AFTER MORE PLANNING, particularly brainstorming what sort of intel would be the most useful and how to get it, the wolves left for the ranch. Teague had given them the keys, and despite the lateness of the hour, they wanted to claim the territory as theirs. Apparently Teague had hired a company to go in and clean it recently, so it wouldn't have decades worth of dust covering everything, at least.

I aimed for the stairs as soon as the pack members were gone, tired of talking, tired of thinking, just...tired. Muted footsteps trailed behind me, and Josh's quiet "Goodnight" to my brothers told me who was following me. As if I'd truly wondered. I entered my room and looked at my bed...and suddenly that first image of Josh lying there, looking so inviting, hit me.

I could have lost him today. He was too fragile, so eminently hurtable—

"Hey." The touch on my arm barely registered, but it was *Josh*, so it broke me from my spiraling thoughts. "You okay?"

I shook my head. "Not really."

"I do think this plan will work, though. And without a lot of violence—"

"I *want* violence," I growled. "They hurt you."

"They did," he conceded in a soft voice. "But I'm okay."

"They could have killed you today." When had I started breathing so fast?

"But they didn't." He stroked my arm. "I'm still here, see? Everything's good."

"What if—"

He cut me off with a kiss.

Chapter 15

Josh

Maybe I was crazy, kissing Drew like this, with his stone lips and shark-like teeth, but I didn't care. It wasn't a gentle kiss, either, but a dirty, hard, teeth-and-tongue attack on his lips and mouth. After a stunned second, he gave in, and I moaned my approval. I hoped I could banish all thoughts of the pride and the damage they'd done, so he could focus on the here-and-now. On us.

"Be careful," he managed after god knew how long. "You'll chip a tooth. Or cut your tongue."

"Worth it," I panted.

Slowly I tugged him forward until my legs met the bed. I sat and he followed, leaning forward, unwilling to break the kiss even for a moment. I scooted back, and he continued to follow, crawling over me onto the mattress. But he stayed on his hands and knees, and I growled in frustration.

"I want to feel you."

He shook his head. "You said it yourself outside—I'm too heavy."

Another growl escaped me, and he smiled as though it was the cutest sound ever. I pushed on his shoulder. "Flip over."

He did so without hesitation, going to his back beside me. Instantly I was on top of him and he moaned in appreciation. Yes, body pressed against body was much better.

"Remember that picture you painted the other night? The one where you were imagining what I'd look like then I was riding you?" A choked moan was my answer. I took it to mean *yes*, he remembered. "Want to turn that into reality?"

"*Yes*." It came out of him as a strangled mess of noise, but his vigorous nod got the point across.

I scrambled off the bed to ditch my clothes, and he pulled off his pants as well. Then I climbed back up on the mattress, retrieved the lube from the nightstand, and squeezed a dollop onto my fingers. Reaching behind myself, I wasted no time in teasing or stroking against my entrance, but instead dipped one fingertip inside. I bit my lower lip as I moved my hips so my finger sank deeper still, and I couldn't hold in my needy moan.

His taloned hands clenched my thighs, but he carefully kept his claws away from my tender skin. "I want to do that for you. So badly."

"I know." But it was impossible. No matter how gentle he was, he'd rip me to shreds.

He soaked up every one of my moans, the glow of his eyes intensifying with each roll of my hips.

Finally, I hefted his dick—which seemed harder than it had been a few moments ago—and tension rolled through him.

"Am I—will it work?"

I gave his length a firm stroke, coating it with lube. "We'll make it work."

125

He groaned. "I don't want you to hurt yourself."

"And I don't want to hurt you." I positioned myself over his hips and smiled. "So if it doesn't work, we'll make use of this lube in another way, all right?"

His only answer was another groan as I held his cock up so I could slowly, very slowly, take it inside of myself. I closed my eyes at the first burn of intrusion, but breathed through it, welcoming it. Not going to lie, it'd been a long time since I'd bottomed—not that I'd been celibate, but usually I indulged in mutual handies or maybe a blowjob. Sex like this took trust and need, and I hadn't found that with anyone recently. Not until now.

Also, he was big. Bigger than anyone I'd been with before.

"Críost, Josh," Drew gasped. His hands were clenched in the sheets, and the delicate sound of fabric tearing punctuated his pants.

I couldn't talk. I could barely breathe. The feel of him entering me took over all of my senses. So fucking *big*. Finally, he was all the way inside and I had to stop for a moment to adjust to the sensation of being stretched beyond fullness.

I opened my eyes to find Drew's latched onto mine, his glowing more brightly than I'd ever seen them. "Move. Please, move."

With a slightly wicked smile, I lifted my hips enough to feel the slide of flesh against flesh. We both moaned...and I gave up all semblance of teasing and started riding him in earnest, slamming down hard. I braced my hands on his pecs as he'd described, digging my fingers into the velvety hardness of his living stone skin, loving the fact that my nails barely made an impression. I could hold him as hard as

I wanted to, without worrying about hurting him. That was such a turn-on.

Sweat dripped off my forehead and fell onto his lips, and his gray-tinged tongue darted out to taste it. He groaned, his eyes flaring brighter. "Josh, I need..."

"What? Anything," I panted.

I wasn't expecting him to lift me up and off of him, careful of his talons, and splay me out across the bed on my back as he stood at the edge of it, but oh yes, I was good with this new plan. I spread my legs, inviting him in, and he didn't hesitate in sliding home again.

I arched my neck, thrusting my head back into the mattress, as he hovered over me. His monstrous features should have scared me—and maybe, at the back of my lizard brain, they did a little. There was nothing human about Drew in this moment. His lips were drawn back, baring his sharp teeth in something that might have been mistaken for a snarl if I didn't know him better. His heavy brow furrowed, and his eyes blazed as bright as fire. He was incredible like this, his features so not human and yet so *him*. And I was the only one who'd ever seen him like this.

That thought, combined with him pegging my gland, sent me over the edge with barely a stroke from my own hand. He cried out as my muscles tightened around the nearly impervious length lodged inside of me, thrusting deep and hard as he came. It could have been seconds or minutes later that he pulled out, leaving me aching, empty, and already missing him.

Was I going to be sore tomorrow? No doubt. Did I care? Not one bit.

"Good?" I breathed, turning my head as he collapsed on the bed beside me.

His eyes were closed. Trembles ran across his skin, like

127

what happened when he was trying to hold onto his human form. "No words."

"Me neither." I sighed and shifted so I could rest my head on his shoulder, making sure I wasn't leaning on the wing stretched out above me on the bed.

As my heart slowed and my breathing steadied, one thought rose above all others. Sex with Drew in his living stone form was amazing, but damn, I wished I could make love to his human form. Just once.

EM WAS PRACTICALLY BOUNCING in the passenger seat of my rental car, a wide smile plastered on her face. I'd made good on my private promise to spend more time with her outside of the salon, and it was clearly something she was excited about. "It's been *ages* since we've gone shopping."

She wasn't what she called a *girly-girl* over much, but shopping made the list. Especially when we bypassed the malls and the big-box stores and went for the little boutiques that lined Main Street. Which was a misnomer, since it wasn't a main anything anymore, but I wondered if when the brothers were last awake, it was. Something to ask.

Today, the street had an old-timey charm, without being historical. There were no reenactments here, or people dressed in period clothing. It was simply a nice-looking street with nice-looking stores in old brick and wooden buildings. Normal, in a way my life had not been for the past few days. Not that my life was usually what anyone else would consider normal, but I wasn't used to having werewolves around or actively participating in some sort of supernatural guerrilla tactics. It was so weird.

It was refreshing to take a break from it and do something as mundane as search for a parking spot so I could go shopping with my best friend, and exactly the reason why I'd suggested this outing.

As I drove along, slower than the speed limit, a motor-cycle roared up behind my rental car and passed, even though there was oncoming traffic. I tried to calm my heart, which had started racing as soon as the engine had revved. Yeah, I might be a little emotionally scarred.

"Jerk." Em huffed. "And did you see? The big bad biker dude was wearing fuzzy claw gloves. Who does that?"

All thoughts of finding a parking spot vanished. "He was what?"

She raised her hand and flexed it as though she had imaginary claws. "Fuzzy gloves. It looked so stupid."

Gloves...or partially transformed hands? Had that been a pride member who'd passed us? If that was true, it was very odd to see them in this district. Unless they were up to no good.

"Did you see which direction he went in?"

"Why? You going to give him a ticket for crimes against fashion, Mr. Fashion Police?" She chuckled, a sound that died away as she realized I'd abandoned my search for a place to park. "You're serious. What's this about, Josh?"

"Direction?" I prodded again.

"Uh, east on Bridge. I think."

I turned and caught sight of the biker in the distance, weaving between the slower-moving cars. "Watch him. Let me know where he turns."

"What's going on?"

"He, uh..." I wracked my brain for a reason that would make sense, other than *he's a were-mountain-lion who's part of a pride terrorizing my family.* "Um, he..."

"You're a terrible liar."

"I didn't even say anything!"

"You didn't have to. I can tell when you're going to lie."

"How? When do I ever lie to you?"

"Right now—Josh!" She pointed in front of us with her left hand as her right grabbed for the *oh shit* handle.

I smoothly navigated around the car that'd stopped in front of us for no discernible reason, crossing the double yellow into the non-existent oncoming traffic and back. "All good."

"It's not all good! What the hell is going on?"

"Can you still see the bike?"

"No! Wait...yes. He's turning right on Wilhelm."

Wilhelm? That was a wooded street with giant, estate-sized lots that followed the riverbank. The houses that backed onto the river went for an absolute fortune, and for good reason. They were sweet. Five-plus bedrooms, water-front, multi-car garages, some with guest houses, on multi-acre plots of land. The neighbors were too close for the brothers' tastes—you could see your neighbor's house from your own—but otherwise, their mansion would fit right in on Wilhelm Drive.

And it was absolutely *not* a neighborhood I'd expect a member of Becker's pride to cruise through. Let alone stop at a house's gate...and get buzzed through.

I stopped a few houses back, pulling over to the side of the road so it wouldn't be obvious to the biker that I was scoping out the house he was visiting. From here, it was difficult but not impossible to make out what Em had called "fuzzy gloves." They definitely weren't that, not with the way they were flexing so naturally on the throttle. The powered gates opened, and he slowly passed them, keeping the revs to a low rumble as he ventured down the driveway.

"What the hell?" I muttered to myself.

Em grabbed my arm. "Josh. What. The *fuck*. Is going. On."

I covered her hand with mine. "It's better if you don't know."

"Fuck that." She jerked her hand away. "You think I'm not aware that there's a huge part of your life you've always kept from me? At first, I thought the secret was that you were in a polyam relationship with all three of the brothers, and you being their assistant was a cover—"

"Em!" My cheeks heated. "I—*no*. No, that's not—"

"But when you were so excited about finally bedding Drew, I knew that wasn't it." She shifted in her seat so she was facing me. "So what is it? Why are you so good at deflecting questions about them? Are they murderers you're helping to hide? Some other type of fugitive? Have they faked their deaths, and you're helping them maintain their new lives? Are you in trouble? I could go on. I've spent a lot of time thinking about this."

Clearly. I felt bad because I truly hadn't given Em enough credit. It had never crossed my mind that she'd noticed the occasional evasions when she asked me questions about the brothers or that she'd spent time wondering what their story was. What our true connection was. Or that she'd worried about me.

It dawned on me that I'd never actually shared the truth of the supernatural world with anyone outside of it. Everyone I spoke to about it—Mom, Dad, my siblings— already knew everything. I had no idea how to even start the conversation, let alone convince Em it was the truth.

But how could I avoid it? My mind was blank. I couldn't think of anything to tell her *but* the truth.

Maybe an edited version? A heavily edited one. Because if I started going on about werewolves and gargoyles, she'd probably call 9 1 1 to have someone take me to the hospital for my own safety.

"That biker? He belongs to a gang that's been harassing Drew." I consciously decided not to mention the vandalism at Rian's shop or my own run-in with them—it would be that much harder to explain why we hadn't reported everything to the cops.

"Seriously? How did you know?"

"The gloves you mentioned. It's their thing."

She squinted at me. "A biker gang that wears novelty fuzzy paw gloves."

I shrugged and made an I-dunno noise. "Don't ask me."

"So they're harassing Drew? Does Teague know? Are the cops doing anything?"

"Teague knows, but there isn't anything the cops can do. I thought by following him, I might learn some more about the gang." I eyed the gate the dude had passed through. "But maybe not. I'm not sure what to make of this."

"Yeah, it doesn't look like a place where a biker would be welcome. Unless standards in this neighborhood have gone *way* down."

"Maybe he's burglarizing the place?"

"Except the gate opened for him, so whoever's inside knows him."

"True. Maybe—shit." The gate started to open again, much sooner than I'd expected. "Get down."

Em and I scooched down so we wouldn't be noticed if the biker—or whoever emerged—looked over, but not so far we couldn't see what was going on. The same biker stepped out of the gates...but without his bike. Without his fuzzy hands too. He was screaming at someone who remained out of view, his face red and his very-human hands pointing aggressively. I hit the button to roll down my window so we could hear what he was so angry about.

"You lying bitch. You promised—" I didn't catch the response that cut him off, but from the shaking of his head, he didn't agree with it. "Does Becker know you're screwing us over? When I tell him—"

Suddenly he bent in two, as though someone had nailed him with an invisible fist to the gut. For a second, I thought he'd been shot. Then his skin rippled, and between one of my shallow breaths and the next, he'd shifted into a mountain lion. It let out a roar, then slinked down the street in the opposite direction from us. Only a pile of tattered clothes left at the end of the driveway indicated I'd seen what I'd seen. The gates slowly closed, silent on their hinges.

"Holy shit," I murmured. Okay, so, following the biker had been a good idea, but also scary as fuck. I jotted down the address in my phone, then slowly, quietly, backed down the street. There was no way in hell I was going to drive past that house now. Nope. No way. I reversed into the next driveway I came across and quickly turned around.

It wasn't until we were near the end of Wilhelm Drive that Em spoke up. "Josh, did I see...did that...?"

So much for my partial-truth approach. Blown out of the water by one shifting mountain lion. "Yeah, you did, and that was what you saw."

"You're so calm about it. Why are you so ca—" Her eyes widened and she smacked my arm. "You *knew*?"

"Hey, driving here!"

She glared at me. "You better tell me everything, Mr. Pallesen. *Everything*."

GETTING through the conversation with Em took something much stronger than tea or coffee. I raided the liquor cabinet for some rum and made daiquiris. Because everything was better with strawberry slush and rum.

I couldn't remember how many times I'd run the blender. Or what time it was. It was still light out, so we hadn't totally lost the day drinking. Just, you know, most of it.

"I can't get over that your family basically pledged themselves to...monsters."

I sloppily waved a hand at her. "Shh, don't call them that. Ever. They're good people."

"Who turn into stone monsters."

"Who turn into *gargoyles*."

"That's what I said. It's not like they're turning into the sexy ones from that Disney cartoon."

"*Sexy* and *Disney cartoon* should never be used in the same sentence."

Em squinted at me. I wasn't sure if it was out of disapproval or because her vision was starting to go wonky. Mine was on the cusp. "Clearly you've been watching the wrong Disney cartoons. But my point...what was my point?"

"I have no idea."

"Oh. I know." She bumped my arm gently with the hand holding her half-full cup. "Your family is good people."

Hadn't I said that? "Thanks."

"But I'm still pissed you didn't tell me all this years ago."

With my system full of rum, it was difficult to remember why I hadn't. Something about secrets and danger and blah blah blah. None of that seemed important now. My best friend finally knew everything about me. I didn't have to hold back anymore.

I leaned sideways and rested my head on her shoulder. "I love you."

"You what?"

That was a voice I hadn't expected to hear yet—what time was it, anyway? But I was glad that it rumbled through the room. I thought about bouncing to my feet and bounding over to him, but that sounded like a lot of work. Also, the world wasn't quite stable enough for that sort of activity. At least he was in his human skin. I wasn't sure Em was ready for the reality of his stone form. And damn, his human skin was *fine*, even in the beyond old T-shirt and ripped jeans he wore. "Yay, Drew! You're home. I love Em. Don't you?"

"Uh." He blinked. "Are you drunk?"

"We are very drunk," Em announced, her voice almost free of slurring. "Because I saw a guy shift into a mountain lion, and then Josh had to explain you're made of stone, and that required a metric shit ton of rum."

I was still processing her sentence, but Drew had no such delay in hearing words and understanding them. "Where did you see a guy shift into a mountain lion?"

"On Wilhelm Drive—"

I shot up. "Oh! I have things to tell you!"

"I guess you do," Drew said dryly. "Maybe I should make some coffee."

"Coffee does nothing to sober you up," Em explained haughtily. "It only makes you a wide-awake drunk."

Drew stared at her for a second, then marched over to the couch, leaned down, and kissed me on the head. He swept his callused fingers under my jaw, and I all but purred in contentment. "I'll make coffee. Teague and Rian should be home soon, and MacGrath and his computer boy are coming over too. Let's get you at least a little more coherent before they get here, eh?"

"Okay." I sighed, simply because being close to Drew was so good.

He brushed his hand over my hair, then headed for the kitchen. I stared after him—okay, maybe at his butt. It was a very nice butt. His back was good too, all ripply muscle under that too-tight, too-thin T-shirt...and his legs...

Em snorted. "You've got it bad."

"He's pretty."

"I mean, yeah, but that's not what I'm talking about. You should've seen your face when he kissed your head. You should've seen *his* face. You're a pair."

I frowned, my thoughts all mushy and unclear. Maybe some coffee wasn't a bad idea after all. "A pair of what?"

"Dorks, apparently." She rolled her eyes and set to finishing her drink.

That wasn't a bad idea at all. I suspected the near future would have a distinct lack of daiquiris. And fun.

Chapter 16

Drew

I set electrolyte drinks in front of Josh and Em before reclaiming my seat beside Josh. He'd already had two cups of coffee, and even if it only made him more awake and not less drunk, according to Em, he was at least speaking more clearly than he had when I'd walked in on him cuddling Em on the couch.

The primitive part of my brain had gotten its hackles up immediately, but the rational part had calmed it down quickly. Josh had been friends with Em since college. She was no threat to me. Us. And being concerned over that, even for a millisecond, confused me. I could kind of understand my possessiveness when I thought of MacGrath, but Em? No. I shouldn't be so possessive of Josh, but it seemed I couldn't help it. Bizarre.

Also bizarre was the story Josh was telling everyone at the table.

"So he was welcomed at this posh house, then thrown out?" MacGrath frowned. "Why?"

"I don't know." Josh sipped the sports drink and grimaced at the taste. "This is going to make me throw up."

Jenn Burke

"No, it won't," I said. "It'll keep you from getting a hangover."

"Says who?"

"The internet," Rian butted in. "Go on and drink it."

Teague raised a brow. Out of the interest of not springing everything on Em at once and overwhelming her, my brothers and I had decided to hold on to our human skins for as long as we could. It was late, and it had been a long day, so I wasn't sure we'd have more than an hour left, but we didn't want to scare her if we could prevent it. I wasn't angry with Josh for sharing the truth with her, especially after she'd witnessed the pride member turning into his cat. Honestly, I was surprised he hadn't shared it sooner.

"And you distinctly heard him call whoever was out of view a lying bitch?" Tague asked, effectively refocusing the conversation.

"Definitely," Em said. "I think he was talking to a woman."

"Men call other men bitches sometimes, though," Rian pointed out. "It seems like something these assholes would do."

"Maybe. But there's a difference when men call another man a bitch, and when they call a woman a bitch. When it's another man, the tone is condescending. Misogynistic. Like the other man is as worthless as a woman. When it's directed at a woman, it's more...angry. That's how he sounded."

"So, a woman. Who had some sort of power over the guy to force his shift." Teague looked at MacGrath. "Alpha mate?"

He tipped his head to one side. "Possibly. Especially with the comments about her screwing them over and if Becker knew."

I tapped my fingers on the table. "But why would she live on Wilhelm Drive and Becker be at that shithole with the rest of the gang?"

"I can't see the upscale folks of that neighborhood appreciating a biker gang moving in," Teague said. "Also...I ran the address through our database at the station. The name on the deed is Martin Garrison." At our blank looks, he continued. "He's about as close to a kingpin as we ever want to see in Arrington."

Oh, damn. That added a whole new layer to this puzzle. "So they have the backing of the mob?"

"Not the true mob," Teague hastened to assure us. "But we're pretty sure he's the main source of drugs coming into Arrington and spreading throughout the interior."

"So we've affiliated ourselves with a werewolf pack, and the pride's affiliated themselves with a drug lord." I shot a smirk at MacGrath. "I'm not sure who got the better deal."

He shot a similar expression back at me, showing a bit of fang. "I guarantee *you* did."

"The question is," Teague said, "does this affect our plan in any way?"

Milo shook his head. "I don't think so. If anything, it gives us another target."

"You mean Garrison?" Teague looked intrigued, instead of being put off, as I'd expected. "We've never been able to pin anything on him. He covers his tracks way too well. We've got suspicions and nothing more."

"Then maybe his connection to the pride is something we can use to benefit both us and Arrington as a whole." Milo rubbed his hands together. "This is exciting."

"Can you pull something together quickly enough to implement it at the same time as everything else?"

"I'll see what I can find in the next few hours. If there's

a string I can tug by the time everything else is good to go, I'll add it."

Josh still had half his electrolyte drink, so I nudged his arm and glanced meaningfully at the bottle before turning my attention back to Milo. "What've you got lined up?"

"Canceling their credit cards. Cutting the power to their clubhouse. Out of the twenty guys in the club, twelve have loans on their bikes that are about to be marked as defaulted, so the repo man will be paying them a visit in the next couple of days. Two others are behind on child support, and their current location will be shared with their exes' lawyers. There's more, but those are the big ones."

"Good job." MacGrath held out a fist, and Milo bumped it.

"Thanks. It was fun. And now I'll see if I can add something in to annoy Garrison, at the very least. Maybe a few noise complaints that bylaw has to investigate?"

In the grand scheme, municipal bylaw complaints would be pretty minor, but it might make him think twice about his involvement with the pride. Though it was still up in the air whether he even knew they were a pride; he probably thought they were a run-of-the-mill gang. At any rate, if his interactions with them were calling attention to him, that would likely make him nervous.

"This woman, though..." I leaned back in my chair and crossed my arms. "My gut does not like the fact that we don't know anything about her. She's an unknown variable."

"I'm not sure holding off on implementing our plan is a good idea at this point," MacGrath said. "I get where you're coming from, but delaying this to get that information..."

Milo was shaking his head. "Yeah, no. Everything's all set up. If we delay, I'll have to go in, reset everything, and then redo it all at a later date. There's a chance something will still trigger at the expected time overnight and then we're screwed with a partial implementation, which blows our element of surprise."

"Okay. Okay, I get it. But I'm still worried." My eyes sought out my brothers. "What do you think?"

"I say we go forward." Rian covered his mouth as he yawned. "Sorry, long day. But I think if Milo can pull something off to affect Garrison, it may also affect her, right?"

"Perhaps." Teague didn't sound confident about that assessment, but determination was written in the firm lines of his face. "Yes, I think we have to move forward."

"Then we're agreed," MacGrath said with a decisive nod. "The plan goes ahead."

Milo did a fist pump and bounced in his seat. "Yes! You guys, this is going to be so awesome. We're going to kick virtual and actual ass."

I was glad he was so excited. Me, I was still going to stew over this mystery woman. My gut told me she wasn't a variable we could simply write off.

———

At five the next morning, while I was working away on my project car in the garage, my phone chirped with a texted thumbs-up emoji from Milo. I headed upstairs to share it with Josh, but he groaned and rolled over, unwilling to even open his eyes. We hadn't done anything the night before—he'd been far too drunk—but he'd still come to my bed as though it were the most natural thing. That's how it felt to me, anyway. Natural. Easy. Easy was good. Easy meant I didn't need to think about it; I could simply enjoy being with him in the here-and-now.

Even if my traitorous brain wanted to jump into the

future, I refused to let it. Why waste the time I had mourning the time I *wouldn't* have?

It took some poking and prodding, but I managed to get Josh out of bed. I drove us to Jane's Diner near the police station, over Josh's protestations, but he deserved a—what was the term?—a greasy-spoon breakfast, and we both deserved a tiny celebration at the implemented plan.

It struck me as I got out of the car that this was like a date. No...this *was* a date.

The thought made me pause. Had the same idea occurred to Josh, or would it, once he was less hungover? Would it freak him out? We'd agreed to explore and enjoy without expectations. Putting a label like "date" on what we were doing seemed like it came with a heap of expectations.

"You okay?" Josh had stopped at the bottom of the stairs leading to the door and was squinting at me against the nearly non-existent sunlight. Today was one of those gray days that threatened rain but was loath to follow through.

I gave myself a mental shake. *You're overthinking, Aindréas.* "Yes. Perfect."

Josh gave me a doubtful look at my too-enthusiastic response but didn't question it.

The server approached our table with a knowing look as she spotted Josh's slumped form. She didn't even ask if he wanted coffee but flipped his cup over and poured him some. "Rough night?"

Josh immediately dived into the cup, so I answered for him. "Something like that. Could we get two specials?" I gave her the details of each order—how we wanted our eggs, if we wanted bacon or sausage, white toast or brown—as she poured me a serving of coffee, and she headed off to the kitchen after.

I doctored my coffee, then looked up to see Josh staring at me. "What?" I asked.

"You know how I like my eggs."

Over hard because runny yolks grossed him out. Was it weird that I knew that? I didn't think so. "Well...yeah."

"And I prefer sausage to bacon."

"Which is kind of strange, but to each his own."

He propped his cheek on his hand, his elbow on the table. His eyes were luminous as he stared at me. "You *know* me."

I frowned. "You say it like it surprises you."

"Sort of?" He straightened and fiddled with his coffee mug, moving the handle from one side to the other. "I mean, I know you guys appreciate me—"

"We do."

"—But this feels different. Deeper?" He grimaced. "Ugh, my brain is too fuzzy. Ignore me."

I leaned forward and kept my voice low. "The last time we made love—" I paused as he wrinkled his nose at the term. "Why the face? Is that too old-fashioned to say?"

"No, not old-fashioned—well, a little old-fashioned, maybe. But it's more that there are connotations to 'making love.' There's a meaning to those words. And that's not what we're doing, right? We're having fun. No expectations."

There was something in how he looked at me, almost pleading, that I couldn't quite interpret. Did he want me to confirm our previously agreed-upon approach? Or did he want me to go with everything 'making love' entailed?

Perhaps what I needed to determine was even simpler than all that: what did *I* want?

Our food arrived before I decided which direction I wanted to go. I pondered my choices silently as I ate, casting glances at Josh now and again to try to read his expression.

He didn't look up from his food, though, clearly too intent on getting the greasiness into his belly.

Once we were done, the plates cleared, and our coffee topped up, I leaned forward again. "Making love," I said firmly. "That's what we did, and that's what I want to continue to do with you."

The way his breath hitched told me I'd made the right choice. "Yeah?"

I nodded, ignoring the way my stomach jumped. The choice was made, and it was good, but there were still so many things I didn't have control over. Like how our conflict with the pride was going to play out. There were elements that could interfere horribly with what I wanted, but I had purposely made myself into someone who didn't worry about the future or dwell on the past. All we ever truly had was the here-and-now, and that's what we needed to enjoy.

"Yeah," I replied. Tentatively, I reached a hand across the table, and Josh latched on to it, weaving our fingers together.

"Still no expectations," he said softly. "If it doesn't happen..."

I knew what *it* was, and I was trying not to think about how it would feel when my time to sleep in stone got closer. "Still fun," I said, "but perhaps we can agree that 'no expectations' and 'fun' don't mean 'no attachments.'"

"Yes," he said, with a tone of heavy relief. "I'm attached to you. Uh, that sounded like I'm a leech or something. What I mean is, I like you. A lot. And casual isn't who I am. You know? Ugh, no, of course you don't know. I just—"

"It's fine. I understand. I don't want us to be casual either." No, I didn't, but my gut still writhed. What I was agreeing to sounded good and in line with what I wanted, but...something about it wasn't *right*. And I didn't understand what.

Perhaps it had to do with the imminent danger represented by Becker's pride. Things weren't yet settled, but they would be soon. I could only hope that once the situation stabilized, I'd be able to determine the source of my uncertainty and resolve it.

Chapter 17

Josh

It took only two days for Milo's hacking to have an effect.

Christopher had positioned some of his pack members as look-outs to keep an eye on the pride and give us some sense of whether our plan was working. They gleefully reported seeing the fruits of our labor. Three tow trucks showed up to repo some of their bikes. There were no lights on in the pride's shithole of a clubhouse at night. Cops took a handful of the gang members into custody and more apparently abandoned their brethren for greener pastures, yelling at Becker and the other pride members from the cab of a pickup and shooting the finger behind them. But the cherry on the sundae was their report of Becker absolutely losing his shit in the driveway while talking to someone on his phone. By the scouts' account, his pride was down to a quarter of what it had been.

I hadn't resisted fist pumping when I'd heard that detail.

Teague reached out to Becker around noon on Sunday, the day before Halloween, and offered to meet with him that night, after dark, at Drew's garage. The location was strategic—it was the brothers' territory, the surroundings would be practically empty in the industrial area at that time of night on a Sunday, and we could have Christopher and his pack hidden out of sight as backup if needed. Everything was all set.

Well, almost everything.

"I'm going." I glared at Drew, who glared right back.

"Like hell you are."

I threw my hands in the air and marched out of my bedroom. For once, I wasn't at my parents' place on a Sunday—I'd begged off to spend time with Drew. They still didn't know about the issues with the pride. They thought I simply wanted to spend as much time as possible with him. The lie sat heavily in my gut, but the truth would only worry them.

"What happened to trusting me to make my own decisions?" I shot over my shoulder as I jogged down the stairs.

"Do you know how dangerous this could be?" he called after me, his stone feet heavy on the wooden treads. "Josh, come on."

At the foot of the stairs, I spun around to face him. "Yes, thank you. I do have some experience with how dangerous Becker and his assholes can be. That's why I need to be there."

He reached the floor and stood there, his cold blue eyes glowing and his stone talons braced on his hips. "So you can thumb your nose at them?"

"You think all I want is to go 'nyah-nyah'? Like I'm a child?" Oh, that hurt. "I want to show them they didn't succeed in making me afraid. But more than that, I want them to see that you, Rian, and Teague don't consider them enough of a threat to hide me away."

He blinked, and for a second, I thought I'd gotten

through to him. Until he opened his mouth again. "But they *are* a threat. Josh—"

"What's the yelling about?" Teague joined us in the hallway, which wasn't big enough for a gathering.

Drew waved a hand at me. "Josh wants to go to the meet tonight."

Teague regarded me for a second, taking in the determination that had to be written all over my face. "All right."

"Críost! Can neither of you see how much danger he'd be in?"

"Would he be in any less danger if we left him here alone?" Teague tilted his head. "Use your logic instead of your emotions, Drew. They'll be watching and they'll want to exploit any vulnerability they see. If they suspect there's a way to avoid negotiating..."

"Then you and Rian go to the meet. Josh and I will stay here."

Teague's pronounced brow furrowed. "That will make them think we're divided in this. No. We all go. We'll have the pack there and the three of us. Josh will be well protected."

The expression on Drew's face wasn't one I was used to seeing. Uncertainty and...fear? "Tadgh..."

Teague clapped a hand on Drew's shoulder. "It'll be okay."

Drew covered the hand with his own. "It had better be."

DREW HAD MOVED HIS CLIENTS' cars out of the garage bays in preparation for the meeting, so the garage's interior was empty. It felt almost cavernous—without any vehicles to encumber it, the space was huge. I'd never seen it empty like this, and it was a little unsettling. One of the bay doors was open so we could see Becker when he showed up. The air was crisp enough to nip at my nose, and I was glad I'd dug out my winter jacket and toque. The brothers, of course, wore their stone skins, athletic pants, and nothing more. The cold never bothered them.

The muffled rumble of a motorcycle cut through the stillness of the dark, and a few moments later, Becker came into view, with a pickup truck following. We never expected Becker to show up alone—Teague hadn't asked it of him—but how many people had he brought with him? I had to remind myself that we had backup too. Christopher, Milo, Gage and the other wolves that had already joined them on this side of the country were hidden. Our aces in the hole, so to speak.

Becker pulled into the garage's parking lot, and the truck came up beside him, bumping over the curb. As Becker dismounted and kicked out the stand on his bike, the truck doors opened and disgorged the pride members who'd stuck with their leader. There were five. *Five.* That was all. Unless he'd left others back at the clubhouse, but I didn't think that was the case, based on the scouts' report.

Our plan had worked. Jubilation rushed through me. We were going to force Becker and his mountain lions out of town without resorting to violence, without—

The driver's door opened. There was a flash of black hair, glinting orange under the streetlight in front of the shop, before a petite woman rounded the open door and strode to the front of the truck, overtaking Becker to approach the garage doors ahead of him. I was standing between Drew and Teague, and I felt the moment they each simply froze. They stopped breathing, stopped moving, just...stopped.

Why? There was nothing overtly threatening about the woman. She was maybe five-two, with a broad hourglass figure. Her hair was a riotous mess of spiral curls, with the sides pulled back in a simple half ponytail. She had long, sharp nails in turquoise blue and a sparkly stud in her right nostril. She wore jeans, black leather boots, and a black leather jacket over a bright-pink shirt with a saying on it that I couldn't quite make out. Other than the possibly too-sharp nails, she looked like a young suburban mom.

But something about her had shocked the brothers.

"The brothers Ó Raghailligh. It's been a minute since we last faced each other, hasn't it?" Her voice was low and dark, unnaturally smooth, with a much thicker accent than the brothers'. I couldn't explain how, but I *knew* she wasn't human. I didn't think she was a shifter, either. She felt too...*other*.

"You," Teague breathed. "How?"

"You poor, daft lads. Thought I was a witch, didn't you? Cursed you and fled, never to be seen again." She laughed, the sound as musical as minor-key chimes, and as disquieting. "The joke seems to be on me, thinking I'd done away with you. But someone messed with my curse, didn't they? Otherwise you wouldn't be standing here."

Oh...oh my god. This...this was the woman who'd killed the brothers' parents. But how? What sort of supernatural creature had such a long lifespan? Vampire, maybe? I'd never seen one in person, but I was pretty sure they existed in a world that had werewolves and other shifters. Though I'd never heard any stories of vampires using magic...

Drew took a hard step forward, but Teague shot out an arm to hold him back. Surprisingly, Drew heeded it and stopped.

"What do you want?" Teague demanded.

"Why did you kill our parents?" Rian shouted.

She casually waved a hand as though that question were beneath her. "They made a deal with me and reneged on our agreed-upon payment."

"Which was?"

She smiled, her teeth seeming more pointed than they should be. "Their first born son."

Teague's mouth dropped open. "What?"

"Don't believe her," Drew growled. "She's lying."

She swept her hair behind her shoulders and shot Drew a glare. "I cannot lie, you worthless cur, or have you forgotten the stories of your people? Your parents sought me out, for they wanted children and could not conceive. I tended that issue for them, but my payment was their first born son, in his thirtieth year, as my husband."

We all froze. Even Becker was silent. I never thought I'd feel empathy for the guy, but it had to be weird to be thrust into what sounded like a freaking fairytale.

"Why not take me, then?" Teague's voice was softer—no doubt he was stunned by this revelation. "Why kill them? Why the curse?"

"They reneged on our deal. When I returned to claim my prize, your mother had the audacity to deny me and yet ask for my skills as an apothecary, *again*." She said it with a tone and expression that made it clear she thought Teague was not very intelligent. "You would have been taken—but the gobshites of the king's army got to me first. And the curse? How better to cause confusion and escape? I had planned to return and awaken you, and only you, but when I did so, you were gone."

Becker shook off whatever disbelief had kept him silent. "This is all *fascinating*, but can we get to the point of this visit?"

Drew bared his teeth at the shifter. "And you? How did you get involved in this?"

Becker smirked. "When a pretty lady comes to you and asks for help getting to three brothers and offers you a city in return, are you going to say no?"

Teague turned his attention to Becker, but he wasn't stupid enough to completely ignore the woman, whatever her name was. "Here's the deal. You and what's left of your pride leave Arrington, and we put everything back to how it was with your accounts."

"I have a counter-offer," the woman said. "We'll leave Arrington once I'm paid what I'm owed."

Drew and Rian immediately moved in front of Teague. "No," Drew growled. "Not happening."

"Your bargain is null and void." I instantly regretted saying anything when the woman's and Becker's gazes found me in the shadows, but she was operating under an erroneous assumption. "You had a deal with the brothers' parents. As you said, they reneged. You took payment in the form of their lives, and therefore, the deal is complete."

She stared at me for a moment, then chuckled. "A human boy dares to tell me how my bargains work? The gall. The absolute gall."

"I'm sure any court would support me." Taking a chance, I added, "Even yours, I suspect. The Tuatha Dé Danaan have strict rules regarding conduct, don't they?"

Her expression darkened. "They might, but I'm not a member of that court, boy."

"She's Fomhóraigh," Drew shot over his shoulder. "Fomori. They're enemies of the Tuatha Dé Danaan."

Oh. Great. Well, I'd stepped in it, hadn't I? But I refused to let my fear show. "In any case, there's your honor to consider. You took payment, and yet you *still* want more?"

"Josh..." Drew whispered.

"Josh, is it?" The woman—or did that word even apply to her?—tossed her hair over her shoulder again. "This discussion is for the adults. Run along now."

I knew she was baiting me, but I couldn't help getting my back up. "I might not be as old as dirt, like you—"

"Josh!" Drew looked like he wanted to leap in front of me, but he didn't want to leave Teague vulnerable.

"But I've acted honorably in my life." Uh, except for the whole fake boyfriend thing and lying to people. "More honorably than you." I glanced at Teague. "There must be a way to tell her people that she's not honoring her bargains. Or maybe to tell the Tuatha Dé Danaan—"

Apparently, that was one too many mentions of the fae folk. The woman shrieked, a sound that was so high-pitched that my hands immediately flew up to cover my ears. Out of the corner of my eye, I saw the window in the front door shatter, shards of glass glittering as they tumbled to the floor.

Suddenly, I was being pushed back, deeper into the garage, and it took me a moment to realize Drew was the one moving me. His lips formed words, but I couldn't hear him, and before I could ask him to repeat himself, he was gone. A fight had broken out—more mountain lions had shown up, but Christopher's wolves were nowhere to be seen. If I'd found the Fomori's shriek incapacitating, it had to be ten times worse for the wolves with their enhanced senses. Becker's pride must have been prepared with earplugs.

Shit. This was exactly what we didn't want, a full-on fight between the brothers and the pride. Drew, Rian and Teague were holding their own—it was difficult to disable them, with their stone skin. Drew swung one of his wings around, knocking an attacker to the cement. A rune carved into Rian's arm flared with the same red light that glowed in his eyes and another mountain lion flew through the air before he could even touch him. Teague's tail wrapped around the wrist of an attacker and yanked the female mountain lion forward. But they were still only three, and the pride outnumbered them. The Fomori had disappeared, seemingly content to have the pride fight her battle.

I remained on my hands and knees on the shop floor as my ears rang. My balance felt off, as though the world was swaying back and forth, and the cold seeping into my palms from the chilly concrete wasn't doing much to help counteract it. Staying where I was wasn't an option though. I was too vulnerable, especially since the wolves hadn't yet shown up to provide the backup they'd promised. I shifted my weight, preparing to hoist myself up, when something grabbed my hair and yanked me to my feet. Painfully.

In an instant, I was face-to-face with a wildly pissed-off Fomori. Her dark eyes sparked with anger, and her lips were twisted, revealing teeth almost as pointed as Drew's gargoyle ones. Her sharp nails bit into my scalp as she held me up with only one hand. She might look tiny, but it was clear she was anything but physically weak.

"You question me, boy? You cast doubt on my honor?" Her words were muffled by the ringing in my ears, but I could still hear the venom in her tone as she dragged me backwards, deeper into the shop. I opened my mouth to shout, but she wrapped her other hand around my throat and squeezed. "You're inserting yourself where you have no business. Did no one ever tell you that calling attention to yourself is a fault of character? Especially when you're dealing with one of my kind."

She slammed my head against something—a shelf?— and let go. I crumpled to the floor, dazed, out of it, but still conscious. She moved around me, but I didn't understand what she was doing...until I saw the orange-red glow of fire.

She crouched in front of me, and it took a monumental effort to focus on her face. She patted my cheek, none too gently. The painful kiss of her talons slicing through my skin was almost too much for my overloaded brain. "It's a shame you weren't taught the proper lessons, boy. Now you'll pay the price." She had a bottle in her hand, partially filled with a clear liquid, a burning rag stuffed into the end of it.

She casually tossed it into a pile of rags a dozen feet away.

Chapter 18

Drew

I'd never say I was a lover, not a fighter, but I hadn't had cause to exercise my fighting skills this awakening. It was somewhat frightening how easily the motions came back to me, as though they were burned into my muscles. My world devolved into the simplest and probably oldest scenario known to humankind: fighting for survival.

It kept me from thinking about the revelation of seeing *that woman*. Who, apparently, wasn't a woman at all. I wasn't ready to deal with that yet.

"Fuck. Drew!"

I whipped around at Rian's shout, thinking he needed my help. Instead, he jerked his chin at the garage. I followed the gesture to see thick, acrid smoke billowing through the open bay door, following along behind the retreating Fomori as though it were her trail. What the hell?

She sauntered toward the truck and let out a piercing whistle. "C'mon, lads. We've made our point for tonight."

For an instant, I was torn. Go after the Fomori, or save my garage? The question was answered when I realized

Josh wasn't where I'd left him near the office. He'd been in plain view through the open bay door the last time I'd looked. All thoughts of pursuing the Fomori were forgotten as I sprinted into the garage, which was quickly filling with smoke. I crouched down, out of the worst of it, and searched for Josh. Had he hidden in the office? Did he not know the garage was on fire?

"Get the fire extinguisher!" I shouted and threw the office door open. Despite the gaping bay door, the smoke was thick enough to hinder my vision. It took me a second to realize I wasn't looking at Josh on the floor of the office, but MacGrath and one of his wolves. They weren't moving and I thought for a second that they were dead; but then I noticed their sides expanding with each breath, and realized they must have been rendered senseless by the Fomori's screech. "Fuck. Need some help here!"

I hauled MacGrath up, draping one of his arms over my shoulders. His head lolled about for a second, then he snapped back to consciousness with a jerk.

"Easy." I pitched it loud enough that he'd be able to hear over what I presumed was ringing in his ears. "I've got you."

"You're not him," he murmured.

Him who? I didn't have time to devote any brain power to the question. I still had to find Josh.

I laid the alpha wolf on the ground in the parking lot and turned back to the garage, noting absently that the flames had all but taken over the side wall next to the closed bay door. The exterior wall was cinderblock, but there was plenty inside of the building that was flammable. Rian and Teague were helping more people out of the smoke-filled structure, the wolf that had been in the office with MacGrath and two more, but none of them were Josh.

Smoke billowed from the building, obscuring the light that usually illuminated the parking lot.

Fuck. Where was Josh?

I raced back inside. Panic gnawed at my gut, but I refused to let it take hold. If I panicked, Josh was dead. It was as simple as that. I crouched down again and focused all my senses on finding him. My eyes and ears weren't as good as a werewolf's, but in this form, they were better than a human's. A second passed. Another. There—over the mad crackling of the fire, a labored breath.

I shot in that direction, using my hands to balance myself as I ran as best I could while bent in two. Far too close to the burning wall for my state of mind, I found Josh. Too still. If it weren't for the breaths moving his chest...

I scooped him into my arms and ran for the door. In my haste, I almost crashed into the column of the vehicle hoist but dodged at the last second. My wing hit it hard, and I winced at the crack of stone on metal. Dimly, I registered that it hurt, but my only priority was getting Josh out of the garage. Whether or not I had a broken wing could wait.

Nothing had ever tasted as good as the crisp clear air I sucked into my lungs as I reached the shop's parking lot. Teague and Rian were in their human skins, probably because of the sirens in the distance. As I laid Josh down on the asphalt, I realized there was one sound I couldn't hear anymore.

His breathing.

"Teague!" The panic that had been clawing at me tore through my resolve to ignore it.

My brother shoved me aside and bent down, his ear hovering above Josh's mouth. "Fuck," was all he said, but it was enough. Immediately he yanked Josh's puffy jacket open, tilted his head back, and started blowing breaths into

Josh's mouth. After a few, he sat back on his knees and pumped his hands into Josh's chest.

Everything inside me froze. It felt like my heart had stopped beating. My brain ceased to function. I could not comprehend what I was witnessing. A blanket of numbness fell over me, and I welcomed it because underneath I could sense excruciating pain waiting for an opening to ambush me. If he didn't make it...if he...

Rian tugged me back and shoved an oversized shirt into my hands. I had no idea where he'd gotten it. I stared at it, not understanding why I was holding it.

"Drew." His voice seemed to come from a long way away. "The firefighters will be here soon. You need to get back into your human skin, brother."

I looked at him, vaguely noting that he'd gotten a slouchy toque from somewhere to cover his horns. Obviously he hadn't had time to cut them down, as he usually did after reclaiming his human form, but covered with the overly large hat, they could be mistaken for a massive amount of hair. "I don't know if..."

"You can do it. Look at me." His palm against my cheek gave me no choice. "You can do it. Deep breath in, hold it, let it out. Come on."

It took a couple more repetitions, but I was eventually able to mimic the cadence of Rian's breaths. I wasn't calm by any stretch of the imagination, but the numbness spread enough that I could force my stone skin back into hiding. I folded my wings with a wince—the one I'd hit on the hoist protested the movement—and shoved the shirt on as the first fire engine pulled onto the street.

Teague was still doing CPR on Josh, but as I watched, he sat back with a sigh and shot me a small smile.

Rian clapped my shoulder, then pulled me into a hug. "He'll be okay," he whispered in my ear.

I didn't know what I'd do if he wasn't.

HOURS LATER, I sat beside Josh's hospital bed, listening to the monitors beep and whirr or whatever else they needed to do. He had a mask over his nose and mouth, and his eyes were closed, as they had been from the moment I'd finally found him in the garage. Someone along the way had cleaned the skin around his nose and mouth of the soot that had coated it, though he still reeked of smoke. Or maybe that was me. Once they'd stabilized Josh, Teague had strongly suggested I go home with Rian and shower, but I'd ignored him. I suspected Teague had thought I would because he didn't continue to press the point but shoved a change of clothes into my hands and told me to at least make use of the facilities to clean up a little. So I'd scrubbed my face and hands and put on the fresh clothes, but there was nothing I could do at the moment about my hair. Not that I cared.

Josh still hadn't woken up.

The doctors and nurses talked to Teague and Josh's parents. The words meant nothing to me. At one point, I thought they had wanted to take me somewhere to treat me for something they called "shock," but I was pretty sure Teague had stepped in there too, and that's when the warm wool blanket had been draped over my shoulders.

Teague and Rian stood by the window in Josh's private room, keeping an eye on me as much as on Josh. His parents had spent some time here as well, but they'd left a few minutes ago to call Josh's siblings. The last I'd heard—or registered—the doctors were cautiously optimistic, whatever that meant. Optimistic was good, but the "cautiously" warned me not to get my hopes up.

What if he never opened his eyes again?

Pain shot through me at the thought. I'd known the numbness would wear off eventually, but I didn't know anything could hurt this much. An actual hole in my chest would be less excruciating. Absently, I rubbed the heel of my hand over my sternum and wondered why I was breathing so fast.

Josh had almost died. Could *still* die.

"Drew?"

Rian's voice came from far away, overpowered by the sound of my heart drumming in my ears. My pulse thundered in my throat, in my temples, and it had gotten so damned hot in this room. Didn't anyone else feel it? Sweat gathered at my collarbone and beneath my arms, and I couldn't breathe...

Something pushed my head down. Or tried to. I resisted at first, but my field of vision started going spotty. Whoever was behind me tugged on my chair, pulling it away from the side of the bed, and pushed on my head again until I gave in. With my forehead between my knees, things got clearer again. Somewhat clearer at any rate. I wouldn't have said I was exactly calm, but at least I could breathe. Even if my chest did still ache.

"Back with us?" Rian was crouched in front of me, his head angled so he could get a look at my face. He was in an awkward as hell position, so I tried to sit up. "No, you're good. Stay there for a bit longer."

Teague was beside me, and it was his hand firmly planted on the nape of my neck. "Stay."

I let out a faint bark, since he was giving out commands

like I was a dog, and his hand lifted from my neck to gently smack the back of my head.

"Better?" Rian pushed himself to standing.

I swallowed and nodded. Teague let up, and I carefully returned to a sitting position, making sure to keep my breathing steady and under control. "What the hell was that?"

"If I had to guess, a panic attack," Teague said.

Panic? I...supposed it was, at that. In the wake of it, though, came a clarity I hadn't expected. "I can't do this."

Rian frowned. "Do what? Stay here? You don't have to. Going home for a few hours is probably a good—"

"No. I mean be with Josh." I shoved to my feet, but Rian caught my arm before I could make it more than a couple of steps toward the door. Teague bodily blocked my way, as though he thought I'd wrench out of Rian's hold.

"Whoa, slow down." Rian tugged me around until I was looking at him. He'd traded out his toque for his usual back-wards hooligan hat, which meant he'd taken care of his horns while he'd been at the house changing into fresh clothes. "You don't need to make any decisions about this right now. Take some time, think about it, talk it over with Josh when he—"

"And if he doesn't?" I gritted my teeth, the simple act of alluding to the possibility that Josh wouldn't open his eyes threatening to bring the panic back to the forefront of my brain. "For fuck's sake, Rian, do you even know how much it hurts to see him like this?"

"Aye, I do."

I shook my head wildly. "No. No, you don't. I'm not talking metaphorically. I mean, my chest hurts as though someone plunged their hand through my ribcage and is yanking on my heart."

Teague's heavy hand landed on my shoulder. "I know, Aindréas."

Maybe he did at that, with his talent for sensing emotions. I grabbed his hand and lifted it away from me. "If it hurts this bad now, I can't fathom how terrible it will be when it's time to sleep. I can't."

"Can't what?"

I jerked my eyes away from Rian to find Josh's open. Bleary but open. His voice was little more than a whisper, hard to hear beneath his oxygen mask, but there.

Thank god.

The fact he'd awoken didn't dampen my resolve, though. "You and me. I can't. I'm sorry."

I turned and walked away before realization could dawn in his eyes. This was better for both of us. Logic told me that ripping off the bandage would hurt, whether now or in the future, but maybe less if we did it quickly before the glue could truly settle in.

Our future selves would thank me.

Chapter 19

Josh

The beeping of the machines tracking my pulse counted off the seconds of this weird alternate universe I'd found myself in. One where I was in the hospital, to start. One where fae-like creatures who set buildings on fire to kill me existed. One where Drew had unilaterally decided this thing we had was done.

I wasn't sure which of those three things I found the hardest to believe.

I had a good amount of time to think about it all, seeing as on top of the smoke inhalation, Ms. Fomori had succeeded where the pride bikers hadn't by giving me a concussion. That meant no screen time. No phone, no tablet, no e-reader, no TV. And that meant I was bored out of my fucking skull for the next day or so that the doctor said I would be here. I had plenty of visitors—Teague had stopped by this morning, Rian had said he would come see me around dinner, and Mom and Dad usually spent the afternoon with me. But when I wasn't talking to someone, or sleeping, I was thinking.

Or maybe *stewing* was a better description. Something

was simmering right below the surface, though I couldn't tell if it was sadness, anger, resentment, or some combination of the three. Honestly, I was a bit disconnected from it all at the moment, thanks to my meds, and my thinking wasn't the clearest. Maybe I shouldn't be dwelling so hard on Drew when I wasn't at my sharpest, but what else could I do?

There was a tap on my door, and Mom poked her head inside. "You decent?"

I rolled my eyes but gave a half-hearted smile. "Only because I've got covers over my lower half. Hospital gowns are not a good look."

She slipped into my room, followed by Dad, who was carrying a transparent plastic container with something that looked like brownies inside.

That instantly brightened my mood. I sat up straighter and immediately started coughing. Goddamn, I was ready to be done with this crap in my lungs. Once I'd recovered and accepted the glass of water Mom handed me from the nightstand, I croaked, "Treats? Please tell me you brought treats."

"Of course I brought treats." This was day three of my stay, and she'd brought cookies yesterday. I fully expected that if I wasn't out of here tomorrow, there'd be some other baked goodness headed my way. "How are you doing?"

Oh boy, she hadn't been happy to find out about the trouble we'd been keeping from her and dad, but she'd saved her lectures for the brothers rather than aiming them in my direction. At least, so far. I expected I'd get both barrels when I was discharged and well on my way to healing.

"I've been awake for more than an hour, so that's progress." I took another sip of water.

"Do you want a brownie now?"

Dad nudged his way past Mom and pressed a kiss to my hair. "He looks exhausted, Dana."

He wasn't wrong. I was feeling better but definitely nowhere close to normal. "I think I'll save it for later, if that's okay."

She waved off my comment. "They'll keep. I made enough for the boys too." Dad settled into the chair beside my bed, while Mom hiked her butt onto the mattress near my knee. "I thought Drew would be here."

If he hadn't broken up with me, sure, he probably would have been. But I hadn't felt like sharing that tidbit yet—the thought of it had been as exhausting as the idea of walking to the bathroom on my own. Today, though...today I couldn't hold it in. I didn't want to.

How dare he make that decision when I wasn't capable of having an adult discussion about it? How dare he walk away when we were just starting to get somewhere?

I gritted my teeth. "You know it wasn't real, right?"

Mom shot a look at Dad, confusion written all over her face. "What wasn't real?"

"The whole 'boyfriend' thing. He took pity on me when I was thinking about ditching the reunion because I didn't have a date."

Mom covered my hand with hers. "Honey—"

"And then I agreed to dinner out with Brandon—god, I'm such an idiot—which of course ended in that stupid scene, the one you heard about, and I didn't have the balls to tell you the truth."

"Josh—"

"And the kicker? I was trying to take your advice and maybe make this thing with Drew into something, you know? Even though we'd started out as fake. And I thought things were...you know. Heading somewhere. Maybe not

166

curse-breaking somewhere, but somewhere. But then the fire and the Fomori, and..." I waved a hand, encompassing everything. "Drew decided he was done."

Silence greeted my last sentence. I squinted at Mom, wondering why she wasn't saying anything. Finally, she crooked a brow. "Are you finished? Can I speak?"

I frowned since the slight smile and the undeniable hint of sarcasm in her voice were not what I was expecting. "Yeah?"

"Okay, first of all, don't you ever lie to me again. That's not how we work, and you know it."

I grimaced. "I'm sorry."

She sighed and patted my hand. "I am too. Looking back, I can see that my reaction would have been difficult to...counteract."

"A bit, yeah."

"But it seemed so *right*," Dad interjected.

Again, he wasn't incorrect. "It felt right too," I admitted faintly.

Mom's smile widened. "You might think it was fake, but honey, it looked totally real when you were over the other night. Drew couldn't keep his hands off you and he lit up when he was looking at you. It was sweet."

"He did?"

"Definitely," Dad said.

"Then why—"

"Oh, Josh, he's terrified." Mom's smile died away. "You should have seen him when they brought you in here. He was..." She shook her head.

"Beside himself," Dad finished.

"Absolutely beside himself. Rian told me he had a panic attack at one point."

"*Drew* did?" That didn't compute. He was usually so

put together, confident and sure of himself. I couldn't remember a time when he'd ever broken down in any capacity.

"Consider his perspective. I don't know if you've noticed, honey, but all of those boys...? They keep themselves so separate. They care about us, that's completely clear, and you in particular, but they always keep us at arm's length."

It wasn't something I'd spent a lot of time dwelling on, but now that she mentioned it... "That's true."

The brothers and I talked, but not about anything meaningful. A good example was the fact that I'd only gotten the whole story of the curse's origins out of Drew a few days ago, and I'd known him my entire life. They didn't open up. They gave, yes, but they never took because they never let themselves be vulnerable enough to need anything from us beyond what our family had promised so long ago: protection and loyalty.

"They have twenty-five short years to do all their living in, and when they wake up again, everyone they'd gotten to know is gone. They have to build all new relationships, which they've done how many times? I think they've learned to hold back pieces of themselves so they can protect their hearts." She smiled sadly again. "Then here you come, blowing that practice to smithereens, at least for Drew."

"I don't know if I'd—"

"Psh. Sweetheart. You can't tell me there wasn't some attraction there."

"Mom."

"What? I have eyes. The way he looked at you..." She fanned herself with one hand.

"*Mom.*" My cheeks flushed and I scrambled to take another few sips of water.

She chuckled. "My point is, Drew isn't indifferent to you. At all. But if he lets you in all the way, and you don't break the curse, and he has to go to sleep again in two years...you won't be there when he wakes up."

Realization dawned, and my breath caught. "And he got a taste of that when I was hurt."

Dad pointed a finger gun in my direction. "Exactly."

"So he's making his decision totally based on fear."

Mom nodded. "Exactly."

"Well, that's dumb." But now that Mom had laid it out for me, completely understandable.

"So." Mom quirked her eyebrows up and down. "What are you going to do about it?"

I never thought I'd be plotting how to rescue my love life with my parents while I sat in a hospital bed, but...let's be real, that wasn't the weirdest thing I'd ever done. My life was all kinds of strange and unexplained and wonderful, and I was going to let Drew know in no uncertain terms that he was not getting away quite that easily.

Chapter 20

Drew

My garage was gone.

I sat in my truck in an empty lot across the street, looking at the skeleton of my workplace, my passion, surrounded by crime-scene tape. The concrete block walls were mostly still standing but ragged and blackened with soot and smoke. The sign above the main entry was scorched, the logo and name all but unreadable. The bay doors remained open, and the interior was nothing but charred remains of things I couldn't identify, at least not from here. God knew when they were going to let me see if I could salvage any of my tools or equipment, or if they ever would.

I wanted to focus on what was in front of me and the anger, the *rage*, that went with the destruction of my livelihood. Or, alternatively, the horror and worry that accompanied the thought that my parents' murderer was still alive and continuing to plot against us. But my brain was having none of it, instead returning to the sight of Josh in his hospital bed. I hadn't seen his expression as I left, but I could imagine him watching me with a look of tired confusion that transformed into something that would have pierced my heart: betrayal and hurt.

An Arrington police cruiser turned onto the street and into the lot beside me. I tensed for a second until I saw that it was Teague. The police and fire department had some significant questions about how the fire started since they'd found traces of accelerant, but I was hoping they would eventually write it off as something that had been in place already. Otherwise, it would be difficult to explain that an ancient non-human creature had set a fire to kill Josh for mouthing off at her.

Teague got out of his cruiser, and I popped open the door on my truck to join him, even though I didn't much feel like talking. To anyone.

"Wallowing?" he said in lieu of a greeting.

"Trasna ort féin."

He chuckled at the curse, grabbed the back of my neck, and gave me a shake. I didn't want to admit how grounding I found the touch of skin on skin, but there was no denying how it calmed my pulse. A tiny bit, anyway. Teague had always been the rock of the family, and that hadn't changed in all these years. I didn't know what the rest of us would have done after the curse without Teague's unwavering presence. He was the one who kept us sane.

"We'll rebuild it."

"In two years?"

He shrugged. "Or we can tear it down and you can work out of the garage at home."

"It won't be the same."

"Of course not. Nothing ever is." His pale blue eyes grew darker still as he no doubt thought about what we'd wake up to in a hundred years. So much had changed this time around: computers, airplanes, space travel. We hadn't recognized the world. The idea of having to adapt, *again*, was absolutely exhausting.

The idea of doing it without Josh? Heartbreaking.

But that was our lot, wasn't it? To go to sleep, to wake up, to never again be able to spend time with the people we'd come to care about. It wasn't fair. I knew our aunt had meant well, interfering with the curse, but the Fomori herself couldn't have dreamed up a better torture for us.

Speaking of... "Any luck in tracking her down?"

We moved to the front of the truck and leaned our backs against the grille as we both took in the remnants of my garage. "No. She's no longer at Garrison's place, and what's left of the pride abandoned the clubhouse. They're still in the area—another officer reported seeing Becker yesterday—but I don't know where they're hiding out."

"How can you not know? Arrington's not that big."

"Big enough for a dozen people to make themselves scarce. Not to mention the, you know..." He quirked a brow at me. "Wilderness."

I wasn't in the mood to tolerate sarcastic comments. "Why aren't you looking harder for them? Don't you care that they tried to kill Josh?"

"Don't be an asshole, Drew. Of course I care."

"Then you should be out there looking for them!" I pushed off the truck and turned to face Teague, my fists clenched at my sides.

Teague didn't move. "We are."

"Josh could have *died*."

"And that freaks you the fuck out."

"Yes!"

"Why?"

"What do you mean, why? Because he's important to us."

"To us, huh?"

"Yes, to *us*! You just said you cared about him."

"I do. But not like you do."

"I don't—" I swallowed. "He's important."

"He's more than important to you."

I shook my head rapidly. "I don't know what you mean."

"Yes, you do." Finally, Teague moved to face me head-on and grabbed both my shoulders. "Come on, Drew."

My heart was pounding. I wanted to shake my head again, to deny what he was suggesting. Or maybe wrench out of his hold and run away from him, from Josh, from the feelings I was trying so hard to keep at bay. But Teague's grip was tight enough to leave bruises if I tried to move.

"You don't know what you're asking." I was breathless, like I'd run here from the mansion.

"I do," Teague said, his voice low, his eyes full of compassion.

Of course he did. My emotions were probably screaming at him. He squeezed my shoulders tighter and the bite of his fingers cracked something in me.

"What if he leaves me?" I choked out.

"He won't."

"He almost did."

"And so you're going to let that fear make decisions for you?" Teague tilted his head. "That's not you."

Except perhaps, when it came to this, it was. I *was* scared. More scared than I'd ever been, even when we'd first woken up in our stone skins. If I let them, these feelings in my gut would leave me so very, very vulnerable. I couldn't chance giving them a name. Admitting to them.

"Drew." Teague said my name so faintly, with such compassion that it almost brought tears to my eyes. "You know what this is."

I swallowed hard. "I can't."

"Yes, you can." He gave me another little shake. "Let yourself think about the future, for once. You don't always have to be disappointed by what it brings, right?" The radio on his shoulder squawked, and he let out a small sigh before releasing my shoulders to answer the call in cop-speak. When he was done, he turned his attention back to me. "No more wallowing, okay? Go home. Tinker with one of your projects. Spend some time thinking about what you want. And try to banish that fear, eh?" He ruffled a hand through my hair, something that took me right back to my childhood.

"Love you." *That* I could say because he already knew it.

"Love you too, deartháir. Do what I said, yeah?"

I swallowed and nodded. "I'll try."

Whether I'd be successful, I couldn't say.

I TRIED to follow Teague's advice. I honestly did. But when I pulled up to the mansion and realized, again, that Josh wouldn't be there, I turned around and went for a long drive to nowhere in particular. I didn't wallow, but I *did* think as the kilometers rolled away beneath the tires of my truck. By the time I returned to the mansion, hours later, I couldn't say I'd come to any sort of conclusive decision on my life. Or my future.

When I trudged through my bedroom door, truly exhausted for the first time in forever, and flicked on the light, the sight that greeted me stopped me short. Josh was asleep in my bed, curled on his side, facing the door. He was paler than usual, and his hair had the look of someone who'd gone to bed with it wet, right from the shower. He wore sweats and a T-shirt, and was lying on top of the covers, so I suspected he'd come in here to wait for me and succumbed to sleep instead. His face was smooth and relaxed for a few seconds, but then he seemed to register the light, and his nose scrunched up.

It was more than a little adorable, but I might as well have witnessed a horrific scene with how it froze me for a second. It was a moment of reckoning, wasn't it? A fork in the road of my destiny. Which route would I take?

I turned the overhead light off.

"Don't go," Josh said, his voice pitched low. It was still rough from the smoke, but Rian had told me the doctors said that would heal soon. A second later, the lamp on the night-stand turned on, washing the room in a warm, inviting glow. He was sitting now, his legs angled over the side of the bed, his hands gripping the bedspread on either side of him.

God, he looked good. For all that he was paler than usual, there was life to his skin again. He didn't look like he had in the hospital bed, small, slight, fragile. I hadn't known until this moment how badly I'd needed to see him like this, well on his way to mending. My heart sang with the knowledge that he was truly going to be okay.

"I'm mad at you." Josh glared at me, and the fire I was used to seeing in his eyes when he protected us from the world at large was there in full force. "How dare you leave me in the hospital like that?"

I frowned. "Like what?"

"Like you're the one who's in charge of making decisions about us. That wasn't fair."

No. No, I suppose it wasn't. "Josh—"

"I didn't do anything wrong. Me getting hurt wasn't my fault. And when I needed you to be there, to support me, you ran."

Teague's words haunted me. I *had* let my fear make my decisions, and it was clear from the emotions in Josh's voice that I'd hurt him. "I'm sorry."

He paused, as though he hadn't expected to wrest those words from me so easily. "Thank you." He pushed off the bed, his slow movements a testament to the fact that he wasn't fully healed yet, and approached me. "But don't think an apology fixes everything."

"I don't."

"Good." He stopped in front of me and met my gaze. "Because you can't do that again. No more making decisions for me, or disrespecting *my* decisions."

That fear I'd been trying so hard to tame rose in my chest, making my heart pick up speed. "But...I was right. You got hurt."

"I did, but it was still my choice to be there. My risk to take. There will be more times like that, and you have to trust me to know myself. Can you do that?"

Could I? "I can try. Is that...good enough?" *To take me back?*

He seemed to hear the unspoken question, and his eyes softened. "You silly, silly man." He cupped my jaw, and I reveled in the touch of skin on skin. I hadn't let go of my human form yet, and I was so thankful I hadn't. Unlike Teague's touch, which grounded me, Josh's touch made me feel like I could fly. That I *would* fly, or try to, if only he asked. "Do you honestly think I'm going to let you run because you got scared?"

I didn't know what to say, but he kept going, his voice as low and gentle as though he were coaxing a feral cat.

"I understand why you ran. And I'm not saying what you're feeling isn't valid." His thumb stroked my cheekbone, and I shifted closer to him, an involuntary movement that I wouldn't have halted if I could. "But if we're going to make a go of this, even if I'm not the one for you—"

"You are." The words burst out of me, raw and real, and I wanted to shout and vomit at the same time.

He frowned. "I'm what?"

I grasped the hand on my face with my own, capturing it to strengthen the physical connection between us. "I thought it would be like a lightning strike, like it was for Finnian. An instant of knowing that *this* is the person for me. But it wasn't. It isn't. It started building slowly, from that first kiss that was supposed to be for show. I didn't even know it since it felt so natural." My skin flickered, my form reacting to the strength of my emotions, and I fought to keep my human skin in place. This was not a conversation I wanted to have while I was in stone. "That fake date wasn't fake at all, Josh."

"What are you saying?" He stared at me, his face blank, and I didn't know what to make of that. Was I baring my soul for nothing? Was it already too late? But he'd said he wanted to make a go of this, of us...

Grow some balls, Aindréas. Take the leap. Fuck your fear.

"I'm saying." I had to stop and take a breath. "I'm saying that I love you, Josh. I'm not sure when it happened, but I knew when I pulled you from the fire that I love you with all I have, all I am. And that scared the fuck out of me. Because if you don't feel the same...if I go back to sleep and lose you—"

He grabbed my head and yanked me into a firm, unwavering kiss. There was nothing tentative in it, nothing unsure. His lips and tongue demanded I respond in kind, and for a few moments, I forgot there was anything else but this kiss with him. The world, my worries, my fears, the flicker at my core that hinted my human skin was about to disappear—everything drifted away, much less important than the heat of our lips pressed together or the tingles that cascaded through my nerves at the feel of his tongue dancing with mine.

Finally, he pulled away, gasping for breath, and I was about as unsteady as he was. He leaned his forehead against mine. "You're not going to lose me," he whispered. "Because I love you too."

"You—" I didn't have time to finish my thought before a sharp pain ratcheted my spine into a sudden arch. Lightning jolted across my nerves, lighting each of them on fire, and I gasped. Vaguely, I heard Josh call my name, but I couldn't respond, caught up in the sensations that negated all possible thought.

Suddenly, there was a *crack*. Something fell to the floor with a heavy thud. Instantly, the pain disappeared, and I staggered forward a step, off balance, only to be caught and steadied by Josh's arms.

"Your wings," he breathed, gazing at something behind me.

I turned to see a pair of folded stone wings resting on the floor. My hand flew to my shoulder blade, feeling for the unwanted, useless appendages I'd carried for so long...but they were gone. It took me a moment to register the sudden lack of weight and even then, I couldn't truly grasp it. A second later, the wings disintegrated into dust, vanishing as though they'd never been. As though the last five hundred years had been a dream.

"I'm—" Oh god, what if I said it and it wasn't true?

"You're free." Josh's cheeks were wet with tears. "Oh my god, Drew, you're *free*."

Chapter 21

Josh

I stared at Drew for a second...then swept in to capture his lips with mine in a kiss so full of wonder it made my heart ache. Against all odds, we'd broken his curse. I could barely breathe with how big my heart felt. "I love you," I murmured against his lips. The words felt good, so good, to finally say.

"You love me." The way he said it, as though it was almost unbelievable, made me kiss him harder. Maybe he'd believe my actions if my words weren't quite sinking in.

He didn't protest as my hands swept under his shirt, pushing up the hem so I could feel his shoulder blades. They were smooth, without a trace of the wings. I pulled his shirt off the rest of the way and nudged at him to turn around so I could look at the bare skin of his back, wanting to affirm what I was feeling. I stared in wonder—there was no scar, no mark, nothing but a clear stretch of skin, which I dragged my fingertips across reverently.

I knew magic was real. That was a truth I'd lived with for my entire life. But this? Seeing the effect of breaking the curse? It amazed me like nothing else.

"Drew..." My throat was so tight I could barely squeeze the word out, but that was all right because I didn't know what else to say.

He spun around and cupped my cheeks with both hands. "You did that."

"We both did." We kissed again, slower this time. When I needed a breath, I rested my cheek against his and whispered, "We need to get naked. I want to see all of you."

He was grinning when he pulled away and quickly stripped off his pants. I moved at a more relaxed pace, not because I wasn't as eager, but because my chest was still sore.

As he watched, his grin faded, replaced by the start of a frown. "Are you sure—"

"I'm sure." There was no way I was putting this off until I felt one hundred percent better. "Lay back and let me explore all that skin."

A shiver rolled over said skin. It had to be anticipation, because he got himself situated on the bed on his back in record time. By the time I was done with my clothes, he was settled, one leg bent at the knee so his foot was flat, and a hand slowly stroking his hard cock.

The sight made my mouth water. Not only the sexiness of that hand moving up and down his hard length so determinedly, so precisely, but all of that fair skin on display. His throat and pecs were rosy and flushed, his nipples hard and pink, begging for my fingers or tongue. The hair on his chest seemed thicker than when I'd seen him in his human form before, forming a vee on his pecs and dipping in a line down his stomach to join the thatch above that impressive dick. The head peeked out of his foreskin, red and ready, a gleaming drop of precome at the tip. As I fought the drool that wanted to escape, his thumb purposely caught that clear bead and swept it around his glans.

My dick bobbed a *hello* at the tease.

"Like what you see?" He had a smile on his face, but there was a trace of uncertainty in his blue eyes. As though I'd find something wanting about his true human form.

Careful of my healing injuries, I climbed on the bed, on my hands and knees over him, and nuzzled my nose against his. "Yes. Let me show you?"

Swallowing hard, he nodded. "Please. Please touch me."

I kissed his nose as a reward, then his lips and chin, working my way down his neck until I reached his collarbone. There, I teased him with my tongue, drawing it along his skin and reacquainting him with how sensitive it could be. He gasped, clearly surprised at the touch, then moaned in appreciation. When I flicked one of his nipples, he truly came undone, arching into my touch, his moan deepening.

Oh, how I loved finding one of his hot buttons. "Sensitive?"

"I—" He gasped. "I'd forgotten."

Smiling, I leaned down to swirl my tongue around the stiff nub and sucked.

It was like I'd lit a fire in him. "Críost, Josh!"

Oh yeah. This was awesome.

I played with his nipples some more, going back and forth between them and absolutely enjoying every one of his reactions. With each suck, each lick, his cock danced across his lower abdomen, leaving wet kisses. I was so freaking turned on that my leaking dick marked his hip with its own. Suddenly, he froze, every muscle in his body rigid and unmoving, and he grunted as warmth hit my stomach.

I almost came right along with him. Fuck, that was hot. "That made you come? Really?"

The flush on his cheeks darkened, but he looked too blissed out to be truly embarrassed. "Apparently?"

I sat back, my butt on his thighs, and eyed the evidence of his orgasm as I mimicked what he'd done moments earlier and gave myself a few slow strokes. My dick was leaking a full-on stream now, and I was so hard I ached with it. "How do you want me?"

"Inside of me. But that can wait."

I was about to protest when I tensed a muscle I shouldn't have, moved my arm too vigorously, or something, and my body reminded me that, *hey, we're not fully healed yet, remember?* So I swallowed down the lie that I was good to top him, and nodded instead. "Next time."

"Or the time after. Or after that." He breathed in deeply, his chest rising and lowering as he let it out slowly. "We've...we've got the rest of our lives. Right?"

My throat constricted at that thought. We no longer had an end date for this relationship. The future—our future—was wide open. "Right. So...what do you want?"

"Come all over me. Mark me as yours."

Fuck, why was that idea so *hot*?

I'd backed away from the edge with the shot of unwelcome pain, but it took me no time at all to find it again. Drew held on to my thighs, steadying me, as I fucked my hand, using the copious amounts of precome I'd produced to make the slide perfect over my cut dick. The look on his face as he stared at my cockhead shuttling through my grip was nothing but a turn-on. The intensity of it, the focus. His fingers tightened, digging into my quadriceps as I thrust and thrust again.

And then he licked his lips. The sight of that pink tongue, eager for a taste, sent me shouting over the edge. I shot, hitting his chin and lips and marking his chest in streaks like he'd wanted. He swept a fingertip through the mess and brought it to his lips. When he tasted it, he moaned, and my cock valiantly let out one last spurt.

I collapsed on the bed beside him, panting hard, but high on the endorphins. My god, I couldn't remember coming that hard. Ever. Our earlier bouts had been amazing, mind-blowing, but this? I couldn't even describe how right it felt. How meaningful. My body, heart, and soul thrummed with sensations that I wanted to revel in for as long as I could.

But then Drew let out a faint noise, one that didn't match the good feelings rolling through me. I hoisted myself up and discovered he had both hands over his face. Hiding from the world.

"Drew? Sweetheart, are you—"

He shook his head. Then nodded. Then sob-hiccupped a laugh as he let his hands fall away. "I'm so fucked up."

I pressed a kiss to his cheek. "It's okay. You're allowed to be. Uh..." I paused. "Unless you're fucked up about the sex. Then we should probably talk about that."

"No, not the sex. The sex was...incredible. Indescribable. I should be happy. I *am* happy." He brushed tears away before they could slide down his cheeks. "This is everything I wanted for as long as I can remember."

I propped my elbow on the bed and rested my head on my hand so I could look at him. God, this man. Did he even know how strong he was? "Yeah. But the thing you thought you'd never find."

"And the thing my brothers haven't found."

"That too. No wonder your emotions are complex."

"Complex." He huffed out a laugh. "That's one way to describe me breaking down when I should be singing from the rooftops after the best sex of my life."

I settled my head on his shoulder, still careful of my ribs and chest. Now that the orgasm high was wearing off, twinges were making themselves known, but fuck if I was going to pay any attention to them. I wouldn't miss post-sex cuddles with Drew for the world.

He sighed as he took my weight, but it didn't sound unhappy. "This is going to change everything."

"That's not a bad thing."

"Fuck, no, it's not. It's amazing. *You're* amazing."

I tucked my head into his chest, embarrassed at the praise. "We didn't even have real—"

He made a *zip-it* noise. "What did you say to me before? Penetration doesn't equal *real*. Don't even go there with that nonsense. I got to watch you come and paint my human skin. That was...god. It can't get any more real than that." He pulled me close and kissed my forehead. "I love you, Josh. All the shit running through my head, all these emotions...we'll get them sorted. But that truth is never going to waver."

Throat tightening again, all I could do was nod against him before I managed to say, "I love you too."

Chapter 22

Drew

For the first time in as long as I could recall, I slept for the full night. Waking beside Josh was a pleasure I hadn't yet experienced, and seeing him all rumpled and bleary-eyed was adorable. His skin was marked with creases from the pillow and sheets, and his hair was mussed. I'd like to say I jumped him, but I knew he wasn't healed enough for that yet. Instead, we kissed and rubbed off against each other in a slow, wonderful dance that put us blissfully back to sleep for an hour or so.

When we managed to get out of bed, we found Rian and Teague in the kitchen in their stone skins. Teague was reading something on his reinforced tablet as he sipped coffee, and Rian was putting together a sandwich. As we stepped off the stairs, they lifted their heads to greet us—but as soon as they caught sight of me, with my human skin and without a trace of my wings, their glowing eyes widened. Rian dropped his knife, and yellow mustard splattered across the lower cupboards and floor.

They didn't have to speak to ask if I'd broken the curse. I could see the question in their glowing eyes. Emotion had my throat in a vise, so I nodded. Suddenly they surrounded Josh and me, hugging us both tight.

"You did it," Teague whispered.

"I'm sorry." My voice was choked up and my throat ached, but I had to get that out.

Rian made a dismissive noise. "Don't. Don't ever apologize for this." He pressed a firm kiss to Josh's temple. "Thank you, dearthair. Thank you."

Dearthair. Brother. We said it all the time to each other, but this was the first time any of us had used it for Josh. But it was true. Beyond that, it was right. He was a part of our family, now more than ever. My partner, Teague and Rian's new brother.

Teague and Rian kissed my cheeks, their stone lips and, in Teague's case, his tusks, feeling oddly threatening against my now-vulnerable skin. They stepped back, swiping at their eyes without embarrassment, smiling widely. The happiness filling the room from all of us was almost palpable.

"We need to celebrate," Rian declared as he bent to pick up the dropped knife and clean up the splattered mustard. "Think MacGrath would let us have a party at the ranch?"

I almost questioned why the ranch, until I remembered that the last time we'd had a gathering at the mansion, we'd been shot at. Seeing as the ranch was farther out of town, and the Fomori and Becker probably didn't know about it, it was definitely a better choice.

Even so, the idea of a party didn't sit well with me. I scrunched up my nose, still finding my human skin, and the fact I didn't have to fight to maintain it, a novelty. "We've got so much to deal with. Do you honestly think a party is a good idea?"

Teague grabbed my shoulder, and I winced at the heft and strength of my brother's grip. It only made Teague smile wider, though, probably overjoyed at the reminder that I no longer had a stone form. "You broke a five-hundred-year-old curse. If that's not worth celebrating, what is?"

"He's right," Josh said, his smile matching my brothers'. "It's a *little* important."

I crooked my head in acknowledgment. If my short times awake had taught me anything, it was that you had to take advantage of any opportunity to share joy with those you loved. "You have a point."

"And who knows when we'll be able to do it, if not now," Rian pointed out. "We've got some breathing room at the moment, but the Fomori will be after us again. Once she and Becker regroup."

Like everyone else, I was disappointed that our plan to smoke the mountain lions out of Arrington hadn't worked as we'd hoped. But then, we hadn't counted on an ancient and determined non-human partner to be the driving force behind their campaign of harassment. Now that we knew, we could determine a better strategy.

Though I had no inkling yet what might work.

"All right. A party it is."

Josh clapped his hands, then rubbed them together as though he were an evil mastermind with a plot about to come to fruition. "This'll be fun. I haven't planned a big party in...well, ever."

"You're one of the guests of honor," Rian pointed out. "Teague and I will plan it."

Teague's eyes widened. "We will?"

"Sure. How hard can it be?"

"Rian. Honey. Sit down before you hurt yourself." Josh

chuckled. "I'll take care of it. Honestly, I'm looking forward to it."

I smirked. "And he wants something better than takeout pizza and chips and dip."

"Hey! I would've made sure we had veggies and dip too." Rian sighed dramatically. "But fine, fine. If you want to take care of planning it…"

Teague mouthed *thank god* at me. "I'm glad I saw you before I went in for my shift. This…this is truly great, Aindréas. I'm so happy for you."

It was getting easier to hear, if the lack of tightness in my throat was anything to go by. "Thank you."

"I've got an appointment in an hour. Gotta take care of these first." Rian yawned as he tapped the horns that curved toward the back and sides of his head to encircle his pointed ears.

"Want some help?" Sawing his horns down so he could go out into the world always went faster if there were two of us working on it. It didn't hurt him; it was an inconvenience, much like my wings were. Had been.

That was going to take some getting used to.

"And keep you from getting sustenance so you can head back to bed with your *true love*?" Rian laughed at my scrunched-up nose. "So cute. No, here. Take the sandwich. I'll be all right on my own."

"Don't worry about lunch for me," Teague said to Josh.

He sputtered, "B-but—"

"One meal of diner food isn't going to hurt."

Josh started to protest again, but I slapped a hand over his mouth. Hey, if my brothers were determined for us to do nothing today but eat and lounge in bed, who were we to argue? I grinned at my *true love*, as Rian had put it, and hoped my devious thoughts were evident in my eyes. "Sounds good. Right?"

Behind my hand, Josh's lips curved. Little wrinkles appeared at the corners of his eyes, which were sparkling. He'd definitely gotten the message, proved a second later with a vigorous nod.

God, he was perfect for me. And now we'd have a lifetime to share, grow, and love.

I couldn't wait.

Chapter 23

Rian

I could admit when I was wrong and Josh was right. He definitely organized a better party than Teague and I could have. The catered finger foods he'd ordered were much nicer than my pizza and chips idea, and where I'd probably have bought a couple of twenty-four cases of beer and called it good, he'd gotten kegs so we could have a selection on tap, plus a wide array of wines and non-alcoholic drinks. He'd even made sure we had fancy dishes and napkins at the pack's ranch, and that the catering company would take it all away so there was nothing left for us or the pack to do when it was all said and done.

So yeah. I could see why he didn't want me in charge of it.

The great room of the ranch's main house had been transformed. Most of the rustic leather and wood furniture had been pushed to the sides of the room to make way for four picnic tables. Each table was filled with smiling, happy people. We'd all needed this break from the nonsense with Becker and the Fomori. But a reminder of that nonsense was in each window with its curtains drawn shut, so someone hiding in the darkness couldn't pick out anyone inside. Just in case there were shooters in the trees, like there had been at the ceremony in our backyard.

I sat at the edge of the room, in a comfy armchair, nursing a sparkling water and letting the half dozen conversations going on around me ebb and flow like the waves on a lake. Half of the pack had relocated now, so there were about twenty werewolves in the room, plus Josh's mom and dad, and Em, his best friend, and most of them were imbibing some sort of alcohol-laden concoction. If anyone asked, I'd tell them mine was a gin and tonic, but in truth, I found I couldn't drink alcohol anymore, not even in my stone skin. My energy had been so low lately, and I slept far more than ever. These days, any indulgence in alcohol sent me straight to bed, barely able to keep my eyes open. It worried me, but it was a worry for another day.

Right now, I wanted to enjoy my brother's success.

He and Josh looked so perfect together. They glowed, as though their happiness had a physical manifestation. Josh's parents stood beside them at the moment, and I could feel their enthusiasm and joy from here. Dana and Glenn had wanted nothing more than for us to break the curse, and I could only imagine how ecstatic they were that Josh had played a big part in achieving that for Drew. I'd heard mentions of "engagement" and "wedding" being tossed around by the two elder Pallesens, which wasn't *scary*, per se, but at the same time, I was glad Drew was dealing with those words and not me. They were big, those words. Giant concepts I couldn't quite get my head around. Mind you, I didn't have a significant other, so...

A yawn caught me off guard, one so big it made my eyes water. The party showed no signs of slowing down, so they wouldn't miss me if I sneaked off to close my eyes for a minute. I left my drink on a side table and headed toward the back of the house, where I'd seen a small library, waiting for someone to fill its oversized, plump velvet chair. I settled into it, thankful that no one else had sought out the peace and quiet the library offered. Drawing my feet up, I snuggled into the cushions and took out my phone. It had become a ritual to look at a particular web page right before I closed my eyes. And no, it wasn't a porn page. Kind of the opposite.

The portrait of Professor Logan Davis smiled gently at me. He seemed like a big guy, though it was hard to tell from the simple, black-and-white headshot. I didn't know what color of eyes he had or what color his hair was, but those features weren't what had drawn me to him in the first place. No, it was his bio.

Logan Davis grew up on the shores of Vancouver Island in British Columbia, where he absorbed any and every legend and tall tale he could get his neighbors and parents' friends to tell him. He eventually turned his passion for folklore into a lifelong learning adventure, which has taken him from Canada's far north to the outback of Australia and many, many places in between. He holds tenure as a professor of anthropology at the University of Victoria.

I'd been thinking about emailing Professor Davis to ask for his help in breaking the curse, but how exactly did one go about asking for help on such a topic? Particularly when there was nothing in his bio to suggest he believed in the truth of the legends he studied. I couldn't count the number of emails I'd started, then erased, since I'd found his contact information via a blog post in my suggested stories on Google. If anyone knew of our legend or had some idea of how to lift our curse, I had to believe it was someone like Logan Davis.

With a sigh, I tucked my phone away. If I ever got up the guts to reach out, would I find him enthusiastic about helping? Or would he think I was out of my mind?

Still contemplating the professor's potential reaction, I closed my eyes. I'd rest for a minute. That was all I needed...

When I woke, I was startled to see daylight streaming through the cracks of the curtains. I stared at it for a second, wondering why neither of my brothers had come to wake me. Hadn't they noticed I was missing? That wasn't like them at all. I uncurled myself from the chair, stretching out muscles and joints that protested being stuck in one position for too long. Then I padded out of the library the way I'd come, back toward the great room. I paused at the threshold, shocked to see all the furniture back in place. Had they rearranged it overnight? Odd that it hadn't woken me. Not that I was the lightest sleeper these days, but putting the room back to rights would have taken a few people. It would have been noisy.

As I pondered that bit of weirdness, Drew appeared on the other side of the room, from the direction of the kitchen. He froze when he saw me, then ran—ran!—across the room and yanked me into a hug.

"Thank god. Thank *god.*" He kept saying it over and over again, and my heart sank with a realization that had been tickling at the back of my brain.

"It wasn't one night, was it?" I whispered.

Drew pulled back and swiped the back of one hand beneath his eyes. "No. It's been three."

I stared at him in horror. "I was asleep for *three days?*"

"Nothing could wake you. The only hope we had was that you weren't true stone."

I collapsed into the closest chair and cupped my head in my hands. We'd known the magic of the curse was fading, warping, or something—Teague had awoken two years before us for the first time ever, and we'd all been worried that he would sleep two years early too. I'd never thought it would be *me* facing that fate.

I wasn't ready for it. I wanted to see Drew and Josh grow in their relationship. I wanted to kick Becker and his pride out of Arrington. Most of all, I wanted to find the Fomori and ensure she paid for killing our parents and cursing us.

Yanking my phone out of my pocket, I pulled up the email I'd drafted to Professor Logan Davis but never sent. Today was the day I was going to change that.

We—I—needed help. I only hoped that he could provide the knowledge we needed to end this curse once and for all.

THANK you for reading *Stone Wings*! Please consider leaving a review on Amazon if you have a minute. If you'd like to stay up to date on all of Jenn's upcoming releases, you can sign up for her newsletter at https://www.jennburke.com/newsletter.

Turn the page to find out more about Rian's book, STONE SKIN, coming in January 2023!

STONE SKIN

The Gargoyles of Arrington, Book 2

Can he break his curse before time runs out?

Despite being cursed to sleep as a gargoyle for a hundred years, and awake for only twenty-five, Rian O'Reilly is an optimist. He knows he can find a way to break the curse through the tattooed runes he's spent years mastering. No need to wait for this true love crap. But he hasn't found the right combination of magic and his time is almost up. Rian isn't ready to lose everyone and everything. Again.

Professor Logan Davis knows about loss. In the past year, he's lost his mother, his twin, his werewolf pack, and he's on the verge of losing his mind. So when he's invited to Arrington to learn about a legend he's never heard of, he jumps at the chance for a working vacation. He doesn't expect to find a handsome gargoyle who needs his help to break a centuries-old curse—and he certainly doesn't expect his grief to finally overwhelm him.

As Rian comforts Logan, he starts to wonder if there might be something to this true love crap after all. He'd give anything to help this gentle giant of a man, but Logan needs time to heal...and time is the one thing Rian doesn't have.

STONE SKIN *is a male/male paranormal romance featuring a magical tattoo artist gargoyle who doesn't want to go, a werewolf professor who needs time to rediscover himself beneath his grief, and a budding love that might be the answer to everything...if only it has time to bloom.*

Available for preorder now!

Acknowledgments

First off, I have to give a huge shoutout to Annabeth for being so generous with her knowledge and energy in providing tips and a pep talk when I started planning this series. Thank you so much for your time and all your help. It's more appreciated than you know.

Thank you to Abbie Nicole for your editing skills! Editors are truly worth their weight in gold, seriously.

Another big thanks to Sadie and Kim for being my beta readers, and a HUGE thanks to Kim especially for being such a great virtual assistant. You make my author life so much easier!

Kelly, your proofreading was fantastic. Thank you for pointing out the Canadianisms I didn't even know were Canadianisms.

And, as always, thank you to my family for supporting me! All my love.

Also by Jenn Burke

The Gargoyles of Arrington

Stone Wings

Stone Skin (January 2023)

Stone Heart (June 2023)

Not Dead Yet

Not Dead Yet

Give Up the Ghost

Graveyard Shift

Ashes & Dust

All Fired Up

House on Fire

Out of the Ashes

Golden Kingdom

The Gryphon King's Consort

The Dragon CEO's Assistant

Chaos Station (with Kelly Jensen)

Chaos Station

Lonely Shore

Skip Trace

Inversion Point

Phase Shift

Novellas

Jumping the Bull

Must Love Dogs...And Magic

About the Author

Jenn Burke has loved out-of-this-world romance since she was a preteen reading about heroes and heroines kicking butt and falling in love. Now that she's an author, she couldn't be happier to bring adventure, romance, and sexy times to her readers.

Jenn is the author of a number of paranormal and science fiction romance titles, including the critically acclaimed **Chaos Station** science fiction romance series (authored with Kelly Jensen) and her fan-favorite **Not Dead Yet** series.

She's been called a pocket-sized and puntastic Canadian on social media, and she'll happily own that label. Jenn lives just outside of Ottawa, Ontario, with her husband and two kids, plus two dogs named after video game characters... because her geekiness knows no bounds.

facebook.com/jeralibu

twitter.com/jeralibu

instagram.com/jeralibu

Made in the USA
Coppell, TX
27 September 2022